Inventing Victor

Inventing Victor

Jennifer Bannan

Carnegie Mellon University Press
Pittsburgh 2003

The author wishes to thank the following
magazines, in which version of
some of these stories originally appeared:
ACM
Passages North
Café Eighties
Radio Transcript Newspaper
The Oakland Review

Book design: Jennifer Resick
Cover design: James Mojonnier

Library of Congress Control Number 2002115404
ISBN 0887483976

Printed and Bound in the United States of America

10 9 8 7 6 5 4 3 2 1

Inventing Victor

Table of Contents

For Fríati

La Perche

JENNIFER BANNAN

At three a.m., we collapsed around the bar. The eve of our restaurant's opening, it was just minutes before the death of Miami's most famous, most obese chef, Gil Stamos. He sat beside me, heaped into his stool, talking shop through mouthfuls of Gorgonzola cheese. Janie, my other partner, *seemed* dead, but then lifted her head for a sip of wine, the imprint of a tile-giraffe on her cheek.

I felt compelled, between my fat, wheezing partner and my blade-thin, dazed one, to offer a sensible suggestion. Tomorrow was the big day, I said, and we should get some sleep. Gil nodded, and lifted his cognac in a toast to us and our restaurant, La Perche.

But then Gil's snifter slipped and shattered on the clay. His belly lifted and fell in ocean-like spasms. Janie raised her head; her stringy hair catching uneven edges of tile. I looked at Gil: slumped back, mouth agape, his great stomach sagging from his body like the yolk of a sunny side egg, the fat holding his arms in midair. I nudged a chubby knuckle and his hand moved rubberly, like a suspended fish.

"Gil?" Janie and I said in reluctant, timid unison.

His last words were, I later realized, "Here's to torturous stools." Poor Gil had tried steering us toward armless barstools, but that was one he lost, having already won many other battles. We were the designers, we would say, don't forget you won the booth war. Gil had been embarrassed in too many restaurants, waiters throwing up hands in exasperation—most tables don't pull away from their booths—until Gil would squeeze himself in, propped and bisected and miserable. He hated booths, and we went with tables for his sake. But whenever he tried for a rematch over the barstools, Janie and I turned him back to the kitchen, reminding him of his place.

We had watched him often through the small, smudged window of that swinging door. His huge arms waved wildly, conducting to the rhythm of his Spanglish commands. We laughed at the apprentice chefs, who watched Gil with horror and amazement, hoping to capture some of his force before it destroyed them. It had been Gil booming in the kitchen and us in the dining room, as we slathered and sponged the walls, rolled out the carpet, installed the tiny fountains in the gardens between smoking and non. It was our best interior design effort yet and we knew it.

Miami anxiously awaited La Perche: where the guilty liberal would submerge said guilt in Gil's saffron perch pottage under the protective arch of stucco and dangling fingers of the spider plant. The complexity of the dishes—peasant riche—reflected the contradictions in the lives of our foreseen patrons. Gil created Brie-stuffed pierogies bathed in young fennel sauté, pastelitos filled with sweet shredded ostrich meat, haluski with artichoke and chervil: dishes people would spend a fortune on in their rush to feel quaint and simple.

Gone. Just like that. Half the money, most of the talent, all of the celebrity.

What would follow is not much of a surprise when you think of who was in charge now: Janie, frequently distraught and always underfed, and me, fearful of failure and eager for a quick fix.

While Gil's family made funeral arrangements, I stepped into the kitchen and laid off the fresh young chefs. They threw caviar-stuffed samosas and screamed: an angry, multilingual chorus. They had suffered an unpaid training period, with the hope of resort-like salaries upon La Perche's opening. But their future here was bleak; La Perche would be no gastronomical success. Gil's obituary took up a half page in the *Herald*: soon everyone knew Miami's most beloved chef was dead.

Hours after the funeral, Janie and I hid from the sunlight in a dark bar in a skeevy section of West Miami. She wept miserably. She'd known Gil longer than I had. She had been close to him, and at least four times she repeated the story of how she'd told him to watch his intake.

"He never listened. He loved food! He loved food..."

I reached across the table and pulled my thumb across her mascara-smeared cheek. "You can't blame yourself. That's just silly."

She looked up in horror. "Tell me, Carol. How can we go on? How can we open a restaurant when food killed Gil?"

I shook my head, thinking hard of how to answer her. I didn't want to be callous. But it was my restaurant too, and now we had the money to do it. Earlier that day, there had been Gil's will to consider. A tired executor in a rumpled suit distributed pieces to family and friends, leaving a hefty chunk of cash to us, with Gil's instructions to continue La Perche. I was surprised (and relieved) there was any reference to the restaurant. We'd worked closely on La Perche for just six months; it had only been named for three.

"He wanted us to go on," I said. "He said so in the will, almost as though he had known he needed to make arrangements, as though he knew he would die."

"Oh," Janie put her hand on her forehead, as if taking her temperature. "He was immensely paranoid of death. Scared the pants off him." She leaned foreword. "Did you know Gil and I were very close? I mean, intimate, at one point?"

This was an uncomfortable detail. I saw how she might think it gave her an edge of control over La Perche.

"Gosh," I said, "I thought Gil was gay."

"Oh, everyone did. That's so funny. Everyone thought Gil was gay. But he was actually very hetero. Just because a man cooks, you know, that doesn't make him less interested in women. Gil was a good lover. He was horribly fat. That got in the way. But he was attentive and—well, tragic. I've always been drawn to the tragic people!" She let loose a fresh batch of tears. I glanced around the bar, but each person leaned or sagged in a dejected way. We fit in.

"We were too much!" she laughed and shook, pushing her fingers into a pack of cigarettes and fumbling. "Both with eating disorders. Gil compulsive and me anorexic or bulimic, depending on the season."

"You're kidding," I said, though I had suspected. Janie and I had worked together on dozens of jobs. There had been joyful moments, times when I'd felt us connect, through the creative process, or through emergency, like when I'd stapled my thumb to a couch. I was often curious about her body, draped under layers of huge clothes. When we met with clients she put on a tailored business suit, and only then did I see the extent of her thinness, and I'd vacillate between envy and revulsion.

Her story drew me in. Where there were extremes, I supposed, interesting things occurred.

"We fed each other's illness," she went on. "I couldn't stand to see a human so fat. But, because we were sleeping together, the boundaries became confused. I would spread my hand over his flesh," she looked curiously at her outstretched hand, "then take it and spread it across mine, and somewhere I'd lost the basis of comparison, and I'd think, 'when I had my hand on his arm, was it covering half his arm, or only a third?' and I'd look at my hand on my own body and think, '*now* what am I looking at?' It was weird, like suddenly forgetting how to do math. I went over that same problem again and again, for months. Eventually I decided Gil and I were roughly the same size. And when you think about it, in the grand scheme, in the scale of the universe, we're *all* roughly the same size." She snorted. "Only, Gil was fat, so I assumed I was fat. And he hated my deprivation; it disgusted him how I'd deny myself for weeks, then go on a huge binge. Finally we were very cruel to one another, and the relationship had to fall apart. But we've always been close friends. We understood each other so well!" She took a yelping gasp and wiped her eyes with the palm of her hand, then swallowed more of her drink. "Can you cook?" she asked suddenly, slamming down the glass.

Neither of us could cook. La Perche would have to change. "Maybe keep the same look," she said. "But without Gil, we need a theme."

"That's what makes it cutting edge," I said. "Finding that gimmick no one's tapped into yet."

We thought and thought. We fiddled with the available table objects: bev naps, cellophane, beer labels. We yelled at each other's stupid ideas: "The customers must wear outlandish hats." "Every table a mini dance floor." "Dishes served in footwear." Then we fell silent and sullen, looking up for an occasional scowl. All the good themes were taken. We staggered from our booth in each other's arms, bumping accidentally into the men's room. "I don't care, I don't care," Janie sang. I sank against the sink and held my stomach, aching from the laughter. She backed into a tall, elegantly concave urinal and lifted her butt, looking over her shoulder at it and shrugging.

"Use the stall," I giggled.

"I want a urinal!" she yelled. "These are lovely, old school urinals." She turned to look at me, becoming quiet and serious, and lifted a finger to her mouth as if to tell me to hush. But her finger went into her mouth, all the way back: her intense expression, the skin of her throat expanding, and she turned to the urinal and let out everything she'd drunk. Strands of water glistened like tears down the porcelain wall in front of her head—something alluring and ritualistic about it. And I went to the urinal next to hers and smelled men's urine and studied Janie and her calm, euphoric face.

I put my finger down my throat and felt the whole day come up and get rejected. It had been quite a day, after all; anyone would want to vomit.

Janie and I were oddly quiet; the sounds from our retching had been minimal, barely heard over the trickling water. We smiled slyly at each other, panting with excitement. Janie ran her tongue over her teeth and touched her fingers to the curved, gleaming porcelain, "We need a row of these in the women's room, propped horizontally, in one long trough."

I was not prone to this kind of habit, but I didn't have anything against it, and it was surely an untapped theme. This new La Perche was an astounding dare, the kind of thing extremists snatch right up.

Janie and I only took a few weeks to set up again. She was convinced she was guided by Gil's ghost: "Oop, there he is!" she would grin, slapping coyly at her behind, as though goosed.

We made no effort to hide the nature of the next La Perche. When reporters called on the phone we announced: "A vomitorium! Gag me with a spoon!"

We rehearsed our answers and had interviews until opening. We discovered we could justify our theme in the self-help terms of the nineties. What we had here was a community for outcasts. And a revealer of societal ills. We made no claims about the fun or excess. We hoped that would be obvious.

"Well, we don't deny hugely fat people the joy of eating," Janie explained to a reporter. "Why should we make bulimics ashamed of retching? Listen, this is a lost art; it was part of royal culture to gorge and purge. It kept a party going, baby. Haven't you ever eaten so much you felt sick, and had to go home before you really wanted?"

The reporter closed in on Janie. She looked at him as though he stunk. He stayed calm under her gaze, though; I had to admire his tenacity.

"People die from anorexia and bulimia, Ms. Fabrizio," he said.

"Our former partner died of obesity, young fella. And for your information, we're all going to die. La Perche will have a very well-appointed smoking section. We're not here to preach good health." She raised an eyebrow, pushed an aggressive jaw at the reporter.

I held my breath. The reporter was a tough one, who flipped the page of his notebook with a determination that said he would not back down. Janie would take the political tack soon.

"The only effect I can foresee La Perche having," Janie said, "is a healthy questioning of the media's depiction of women. We bring back public purging, we discover just how many women are using it in their quest for an unrealistic beauty ideal." She jumped up and threw back her blazer, her ribs and hip bones slicing the liquid green silk of her dress. She jerked her chin in the direction of the photographer, who leaned on a tulled column. "Take a picture, boy!" she yelled. He snapped to attention. Both he and Janie yanked their bodies in contortions as he got his series of shots. It was a stark, post-modern dance, yards of space dividing them.

She sat. The photographer looked at the lens of his camera, as if worried the sudden action might have changed it. He blew on the lens, then took a handkerchief from his pocket and wiped his forehead.

"Bringing secrets into the open serves the tradition of discussion," I resumed. "You'll find it repugnant when first thinking of it, but people everywhere *do* purge. And they deserve a community."

We settled on an all-you-can-eat menu at seventy dollars per person. The idea was that customers would stay all night. We found a friend of Gil's who liked the idea. He was a creative chef, named Rico, and didn't have trouble thinking about which ingredients worked best coming back up: mildly flavored and damned good-looking. Some dishes spiraled a foot into the air. The more outlandish the better, we figured. It would be boring to eject everyday fare.

Janie focused all her energies on the women's room. The men's room had the same layout—a raised circle of porcelain troughs—but the ladies' room had all the extras. Overstuffed pink couches, tanks brimming with exotic fish, tasseled rugs and pillows, gold plated fixtures, live tropical birds. Janie insisted on an attendant, too, though it was an expensive position to fill. We needed someone with an iron gut.

We found Andrea, a reformed bulimic researching eating disorders at the University of Miami. In her timid voice she admitted that she was nostalgic for champagne and strawberries the second time around. We worked up a cocktail hour honoring these ingredients and named it *Andrea's Fault*. She proved strong and kept her promise to refrain from converting anyone. She was there to build up her willpower, to do her research. And to work—passing out plush towels and disposable La Perche toothbrushes, helping women choose the perfumes and oils that best went with their body chemistry, and listening to the countless stories: "Once I ate five tins of sardines in mustard, then washed them down with a gallon of Rocky Road, followed by..."

We'd predicted a community and there was one. I hadn't seen anything like it since the eighties, when cocaine had been the bathroom catalyst for female bonding. The women hugged and kissed, wiped each others' mouths, talked and cried, held onto each other and laughed.

We were in all the gossip pages, most notably *Celebrity Pulse*: "NOT!" the headline read, above a cover photo of the skeletal Marla Strider emerging from La Perche's restroom. Indeed, much of our clientele seemed to have scant room for pumping blood vessels.

People came from all over the country. All over the world. Soon, the everyday bulimic stayed at home. Only the glamorous ones came, surrounded by their entourage of dancers and camera people. We granted a music video channel permission to film a dance show there, but when they wanted the women's room for the dance floor, Janie barked at them to get out. They settled on the dining room, and a squirrelly, fidgety deejay character stood at the bathroom door making jokes at the camera about the goings-on inside. He caught Ashley Franse, star of the sitcom *Pals,* by the arm as she came out. Janie and I howled later at the footage of Ms. Franse wiping her mouth and shaking her hips. "I love it we don't have to hiiiiide anymore! Everybody wants a piece of this," she jerked her bony body in neon blue spandex, "but there's such deniiiiial as to how I got here. Not anymore, thank God, praise La Perche!" She pointed her finger at the camera and quickly shoved it in her mouth, bulged her eyes, pulled out the finger and laughed maniacally. "Gotcha!"

We didn't allow cameras into the restrooms, and entering them from what had become a teeming, disco-like dining room was a culture shock: the lack of flashes caused an anticlimax, so we turned down the bathroom lights and installed strobes. We didn't want anyone losing their nerve because of a change in scenery: it was a continuum, a long, extended party.

A Warhol protege gave us cheap rates (knowing it would make him famous) on two huge restroom murals—one of a naked Gil lounging on a Caesar-like divan popping grapes into his purply-round lips and looking over the room as if we'd interrupted his lunch. Janie burst into tears at its unveiling; at the same moment a herd of vomiters lurched in and gripped bony fingers on the cold porcelain: a great group retch. On the opposite wall appeared a woman representing a mix of female anorexics. Many thought she was the famous Ms. Strider, some thought the singly named celebrity Ariana; I was convinced it was Janie herself. The difficulty in identifying her was because she stood near the ceiling, on a terracing of Lean Cuisine and Tampax, a geometrical structure resembling a sadistic staircase. She haunted us from far atop this conquered mountain. Her arms reached into the air—she was naked and skeletal but her face was large and beautiful, her eyes like two smoky sinkholes. Art critics came from New York and said the murals were like Warhol's stands of Brillo boxes, but more apocalyptic. The artist immediately had his own shows in the best galleries. He sent us letters with lipstick kisses on them. His La Perche murals became a Miami must-see, and the hordes moved in. There were guided tours during off-hours, and the party resumed at night. Prices went up and up.

We took it all in and we pushed it back out. Then we had room for more. It could never end.

There were frustrations, of course, little glitches to get around. Anyone who looked to be less than seventy pounds was turned away at the door. Andrea was instructed to limit the binges to three a night per customer. If a customer went too far, though, we usually had the help of Drunk Doctor Dirk, a regular, who sobered up at the drop of the hat and could get a bad case stabilized muy pronto. The paramedics knew to pull up to the back door when called, and I would wait with a problem purger in the humidity, in the quiet, under the stars and palms. I would press a cold, rose-scented cloth to her forehead and tell her she would be fine, she would get help, she was pretty. It couldn't be all good. We had expected that.

"Don't use the goods!" we warned the servers against purging. But after the fifth fainting waitress we quit hiring women. They were more susceptible to the lures of the party. And it was hard to be stern with Janie around, biggest bingeing junkie of all.

Even I sometimes partook. Tedious chores with the paperwork team or meetings with Rico's kitchen staff were often too ironic to bear. It was like all of us but Janie ignored the truth of the establishment, pretending our business savvy was what made La Perche happen, when really it was the excess, the utter sin. So sometimes I'd indulge, gliding onto the dining room floor to chat with some woman I'd seen in the movies, her flamboyant boy dancers pulling me from my chair to dance—sort of—more like they threw their legs around and behind me, an endless switching of legs. Then I'd sit sweating and grinning and a towering dish would land like a UFO before me, one of my gorgeous waiters would plant a kiss on my cheek and say he was glad to see me having fun. And we would smile glibly at each other—the celebrity woman and I—and dig in, just eat and eat. It's fantastic, how much you can shovel in when you know there's no obligation to keep it. Tossing back one peach margarita after another. Shoving in pastries light as air, cheese squares heavier than bricks, reaching for bread and jamming in a whole soft loaf. Finishing a third potato lobster souffle and ordering two desserts—a caramel flan and a fruit tower with amaretto tuile—licking up the sauce of cherries and butter and winking over the rim of your plate at your new friend. No obligation. No warning voices in your head—"You'll be sorry, you'll be sick tomorrow"—none of that. You go all the way and beyond. That's the point.

And drunk and sweating and full, so full, I stumble into the women's room and Andrea holds out a peacock feather and smiles, whispering, "Watch out, don't get hooked," and I wave her away and look up at Gil, that Bacchus, that belly, then across the flashing room and up to Janie, that hedonist, those bones. . .

"I saw Gil's ghost last night," she whispers in my ear.

"Uh?" I can hardly speak, stuffed to the gills. The room spins with the people, the sounds of retching like the satisfied groans of America's fathers rising from their dinner tables.

She turns me around and kisses me full on the lips. This is no lovers' kiss, as Janie and I have no room for that in our full, full lives. She kisses me again and I taste everything that has ever passed her lips and ever will. Those sweet acid lips of sin and success.

"You know what Gil said?"

"What?" I pull her waist to me, feel I can put my hand around it. She makes me feel thin by association, like Gil used to make her feel fat. "What'd he say?"

"He said it made *him* want to throw up."

I squeeze a smile into my fullness.

"He said never give up. Never let it end. Do you know what that means, Carol? Think of the disposable La Perche toothbrushes."

"We've made some money on those."

"Oh, Carol, let's go all out! I can see La Perche furnishings—use them for a year and throw them away. The La Perche dating service. No hard feelings when your date turns you in for another. La Perche is the brand of the disposable income. The brand of excess. I can see the ads, with people begging the camera, 'La Perche Us!'"

"Ha ha."

"What, Carol? What?"

"No. It's good. Puns are hot right now. Listen, you go ahead and do it. I'll watch the restaurant. You go ahead."

Then, Janie drifting away, my hands on the porcelain, the clean, sparkling rush of the water below me, I ready myself. But for some reason, despite the noises of retching, despite my splitting sides, I can't throw up. The most I can muster is a halfhearted burp. I can't do it tonight. And I don't know if I'll ever be able to again.

I have tasted success – in both directions – and it's not half bad. Still, I can't go any further. I can't follow Janie for another minute. Am I a stick in the mud? A first-rate bore? I'm not sure.

But tonight it seems wise to turn my back on La Perche and go home. To sit down by myself in the quiet — and digest.

We Said Mother

JENNIFER BANNAN

We said "Mother" a lot. We dragged out the word into a moan, scrunched up our faces, shook our heads, slapped tired young hands against our foreheads. We said, "We can't wear those crazy outfits, everyone at school will laugh." We said, "Please, please don't go to the parent-teacher meeting. We don't *want* detailed anatomy diagrams in our textbooks." We said, "No, no, we don't want a birthday party this year." We feared that she would serve outlandish French hors d'oeuvres to our friends who wanted ice cream. We marveled at her ridiculous political ideas spouted over the dinner table; we worried about what she wore to the grocery store.

When we could, we avoided her. Once we understood what a normal mother should be, we never brought another playmate into the house. The older ones taught the younger among us how to keep quiet about her.

And when we had grown, had found our own niches in life — one doctor, a homemaker, a teacher, a tailor and a lawyer — we silently cursed her for all that was unpleasant in our lives.

We had dinner parties often, made close-knit by our mutual complaint.

"Do you remember the giant pink polka-dot hat? That wedding she wore it to, dragging us along? Or the time she swam in the Peterson's pool fully clothed?"

"Was she drunk?"

"No, Mother never drinks."

"Ah, yes, that's right. She never drinks."

"Do you think she does drugs? The over-the-counter sort perhaps?"

"No, I don't think so."

"But perhaps she's insane? Do you think she might be?"

"But, really. She hasn't hurt anyone."

"Yes, but why should we put up with it? I called just the other day, and she wouldn't believe it was me. It took some convincing her."

"Yes, but how often do you call?"

"I make a point of calling once a month. Just to see how she's getting along."

"We should all make the point of *visiting* her more often. She lives within an hour of all of us."

"Now listen, I love Mother. We *all* do. But who has the time for her nonsense, really? The last time I went to see her, just about a year ago, she had fifty rabbits and a pit bull living with her. I swear to it."

"How did *we* come out all right? I know I always ask that question. But how did we come out all right?"

"Must be some psychology to it."

"Definitely in spite of her, I always say."

"In spite of her, no doubt."

We agreed to visit her on her seventieth birthday. We made pies and cakes. We bought extravagant gifts. We met in a grocery store parking lot and drove together, none of us wanting to arrive first, forced to sit alone with her. We complimented each other on our choice of dress and we were on our way. We pulled into her driveway at noon. She waited for us on the front porch, a glass of something purple in her hand. She wore great gobs of blue eyeshadow, perfect circles of coral rouge on her cheeks. Large, lop-eared rabbits sat on the porch steps, under her chair, in her lap, on her shoulders.

We said, "Hello, mother." She nodded. As she stood, we gasped at the sight of her dress, which seemed to come alive like an unsteady, sickly animal. It was another of her creations. Giant hoops began at her waist and encircled her body down to her feet. Six hoops, at least, with only a thin floral piece of cotton material covering them. The hoops gouged the material like protruding bones, sending a chill through us all.

"What a lovely dress," we said, having vowed to be kind.

She guided us inside.

Mother had been making furniture coverings: the material ranged from rich brocades to cheap striped sheets, and she planned to put all the different patterns on the furniture in the living room. Others were ready for the bedrooms, she said. Upstairs. As the pit bull nuzzled our crotches, we noticed sparrows, finches and other small birds whizzing about the house freely. She claimed to have trained them to relieve themselves in their cages. At least one of us, however, found a dropping.

Some of us were allergic to the animals, and suggested that we carry the party to the backyard. Mother agreed and led us outside, where we found the washing machine, a gift from us last Christmas, tossing and turning in a frightening dance, clanging and banging with maddening volume, right in the middle of the yard. Some of us became angry and could not hold back. "Why, the thing will rust out there, Mother!" Some of us inspected the extension cord she had running from the house, and though it was sturdy, we shook our heads. Feeling that it might be best to attack the situation from her perspective, one of us, the sly tailor, said, "The dog might trip over this cord, mother."

Mother shrugged and the dog whimpered.

One of us, the homemaker, opened the lid to see what made the terrible noise. A horrid, grave-like odor moistened our noses and the lid came down. "A giant rock-tumbler," we realized aloud, and the homemaker shut the thing down.

In the quiet, we looked in wonder at her lawn, noticing that Mother had used her smooth, colorful rocks to arrange a stony walk from the house to the machine. The flat, smooth stones encircled the appliance, as if it were a sacrificial altar.

The perimeter of the yard was strangely segmented. One square of it was covered in gravel, with plastic pink flamingos frozen in their tentative steps. Another square held a cactus garden, with flamboyant pink blooms. Orchids hung and curled above the square of yard from which the oak tree grew. Every section of the yard had a different theme: one with geometrically cut shrubs, another with a bonsai collection, and yet another overgrown with vines and weeds. Her polished stones divided each section, reminding some of us of children who refuse to let their peas and potatoes touch their meat.

We sat down at the concrete slab square, on the hot-pink patio chairs. We sliced into the pies and cakes and handed mother our gifts. She seemed not to appreciate them as she should have, though she did smile. We bit our lips and straightened our clothing as she carefully rewrapped each package, explaining that she couldn't bear to leave the artful wrappings ruined.

It was going rather well. We chatted as casually as we could.

She nodded and smiled and patted her rabbits. The allergic among us occasionally sneezed.

Then suddenly it happened. One of us, the doctor, had had too many glasses of wine. Looking around the yard with an amused smile, he said, "You really are nuts Mother, you know?"

"How so?" she asked, smiling back at us.

"Well, this lawn. Oh, it's just," we all laughed nervously as he continued. "It's simply crazy. I wonder how we'll ever be able to sell the house when you're gone."

We silently chastised ourselves for this heartless comment.

"No, no, that isn't a problem at all," said the lawyer, trying to save the situation before it slipped out of our control. "Why, I have a friend in real estate, who says he can sell about anything, at the right price."

"Of course, most prefer to do their laundry indoors," said the homemaker among us. We nodded together.

"I like my yard," Mother said. She helped herself to another piece of pie. We watched her eat, and could find nothing unusual about the bites she took or the pauses between them. Mother seemed undisturbed by us, which was not altogether relieving. How we wished just once we could shake some sense into her. Perhaps, we thought, it would be worth hurting her feelings.

"Mother," said the tailor. "Do you remember the clothes you used to make for us? Those silly outfits."

"Oh, but they were well-made," said the homemaker. "I've used those same get-ups for my children's Halloween costumes."

"Very sturdy," the tailor answered, and we all hummed in agreement. "I think much of my sartorial knowledge came straight from you, Mother."

"Probably," Mother said. "Don't go thinking you're all so very different from me."

"Ha ha!" laughed the doctor, and we all held our breaths. "Thank goodness I don't go around treating my patients with tree bark and horseradish body packs!"

"That's an ancient remedy. You never had the flu for more than a few days when I gave you the body packs," Mother said. She picked crumbs off her dress and it wobbled around her.

"Ha ha! No one ever has the flu for more than a few days!"

"My youngest had the flu for a full six days last October," said the homemaker, fed up with the doctor's behavior.

"Yes, really," yelled the lawyer, "there have probably been no studies to disprove the medical viability of a tree bark and horseradish body pack!"

We glared at each other.

"This is ridiculous," said the doctor.

We sat back in our chairs and folded our arms.

"We don't have to be rude to one another," the doctor continued. "Mother hasn't got any substantial amounts of money. There will be no big winners in her will." The doctor turned and looked at her. "No one among us ever defends you when you're not present."

Mother picked up a gift and began to unwrap it again. We watched, unable to speak. She pulled out the small glass figurine of a swan. She stood and moved toward the bonsai garden. "I think it looks nice here, don't you?" Mother asked, placing the figurine amongst the tiny trees.

"Wonderful!" the doctor cried, jumping up and knocking over a chair. "That is a valuable piece. Oh, well, I should have expected it, I suppose. You have no concept of value, Mother. When I think of my childhood, of the way all of us grew up, I think I should see about charging you with negligence."

"Oh, no, that would never hold up in a court of law," said the lawyer.

"And what would be the point?" asked the tailor. "We've all come out all right, haven't we?"

"Yes, that's true," we said, thinking it over. We smiled at each other and looked over at mother admiring her swan amongst the bonsai trees.

"Mother," one of us said, "we've all come out just fine. We're very successful people."

"Yes, we've got plenty of money."

"Nice houses, every one of us."

"We belong to the country club."

"And the city council."

"We're patrons of the arts."

"We're really very happy."

"And we've all kept in touch."

"Mother? We're just fine, despite you, Mother."

"Mother?"

She turned toward us, put her hands on her hips, leaned forward, wiggled her nose, slanted her eyes, and said, "Muth-errr," in a long, jeering whine. She sounded like a hateful five-year-old child.

Our mouths hung open. Then, our old mother squeezed her eyes shut and stuck out her tongue. We watched in fascination as the tongue shimmered in the brightness. She stood that way for a full thirty seconds, then turned around to calmly stroke her tiny trees.

We were silent for a moment. We looked around at each other and shook our heads in disbelief. "Mother," one of us said. We all got up and walked over to her, hoping we could get her up to her bedroom for a nap. But when one of us reached over and touched the coils of her dress, she turned around quickly and growled. "Go home. All your unhappiness makes me tired."

"But, that's just *it* mother. Everything's fine. We're perfectly all right."

"Hmmm," she said, turning back to her plants.

An unease began to fill us. It was a dark feeling that we very much wished to release. We looked at each other as though trying to pass the feeling around. But we all felt the burden of it. No one could get relief from the heavy weight of it.

Again our mother said, "Hmmm."

Inventing Victor

"We know, Dacia." Gloria looked at me squarely. She was holding a tater tot in front of her face, emphasizing each word with it. "We know it's a lie. We know there's no Victor."

My heart raced. I felt queasy and the smell of the cafeteria wasn't helping. I kept a blank face. Minita was pushing corn around with her plastic fork-spoon, not looking up. "Diego saw you at your house this weekend. He saw you when he came over to feed my dog," she said quietly.

"You were out on the front yard with your mother." Gloria popped the tater tot into her mouth. She nodded at me as she chewed. "You didn't go to Paris. You didn't go to no fancy parties."

I spoke carefully. "Victor couldn't make it. He had to go to his cousin's quínce on—"

"Cut the shit, man. I been thinking about this for a long time. You lie out your ass, Dacia. Every time we want to meet Victor, something happens, man. He's busy, he embarcated you, his Porsche is broken, whatever. It's all crap! Where the hell are these mink coats and jewelries and everything you always talking about? It's a lie, man. You," she made circles around her ear with her finger, "you're messed up. You know, psycho*log*ically."

Minita looked at Gloria. "Be quiet, Gloria." She sounded as if she were about to cry. "Please. Let's just forget it."

"No, man. I ain't forgetting anything. We're supposed to be friends. You don't lie to your friends."

I invented Victor when Minita started going out with Diego. Minita and I had grown up together. We lived across the street from each other. By the time she hit fourteen she was beautiful. All the guys at school were in love with her. Sometimes I think I was too. I watched her all the time, wished I could look as pretty as she did in a miniskirt, wished people noticed when I walked in a room like they noticed her.

Diego went to Miami Dade, a junior college. He was such a nice guy; everyone loved him. It killed me that Minita's parents let her date at fourteen, much less date a college student.

My parents were strict, overbearing, old-fashioned Cubans who wouldn't let me date without a chaperone. I chose not to date, rather than risk that embarrassment. It wasn't like there was a demand for me in the junior-high dating world. I was ugly.

So when Minita started dating I was hurt. I was jealous and angry. I had to top her. If I didn't prove myself somehow, I'd lose her.

We were sitting in my kitchen making a rape note out of letters cut from magazines. We were going to put it in Sylvia Hernandez' locker. It was my idea. Sylvia was such a dip. She was one of those girls who thought it was cool to play dumb around guys. She could always be found in the bathroom, putting on black liquid eyeliner and talking about her period. She'd never really done anything to me. But I thought she needed something to think about. Somehow, I talked Minita into it. These kinds of things excited her, but she always felt guilty.

"So," I said, "I have a boyfriend."

She slammed down her scissors, and her mouth dropped open. "Since when?"

"This weekend I was with my cousin at Miami Beach. They introduced me to him. His name is Victor. He's a senior at Belen Prep." I leaned over my scissors, pretending to be very into cutting out a letter.

"What's he look like?" She was bouncing up and down in her chair.

"He's cute. He's dark and tall. He's Cuban. His last name is Puentes."

"Oh my God!"

"He has a Porsche."

"No way, man."

"Minita, he's filthy rich. This Porsche is incredible."

"What color?"

"Red. Candy apple."

She slumped back in her chair, a giant smile on her face. "I can't believe it. I'm so happy." She got up and hugged me. She smelled like shampoo.

"Did you kiss him?" She sat back down and pasted a bright red "Y" on the note.

"Yeah."

"¡Coño! On the first date?"

"It wasn't even a date, man. We were on the beach with my cousins. We went to one of those life guard booths and went at it."

"Don't go too fast with him, Dacia."

"We're going to a club this Saturday."

"A club? How're you gonna get in?"

"I'm going downtown to that place where they make fake IDs. Only seven dollars."

"That's right. I heard about that. I'm going with you. Diego always wants to go drinking and I can't. He hates that." She shook her head and pasted another letter down on the note.

It was so easy. She believed everything. Just like that, our relationship had been transformed. We were talking about our boyfriends. She had been avoiding that because she didn't want to rub it in that I didn't have a boyfriend.

My grandmother shuffled in. She got herself a glass of water and stood looking down at the colorful note.

"¿Que és?"

"Para la clase del arte," I said.

She nodded and left the room.

"You think she believes that, Dacia?"

"She can't read English. Don't worry, man. We're not gonna get caught."

Minita held it up and read aloud, "*I'm watching you. You can't get away. You know you want it. Can't wait to hear you squeal.*" She giggled guiltily.

"She's gonna shit," I said.

In junior high, everybody wrote notes. Sometimes they were up to three pages long. They were always folded in elaborate shapes but generally said nothing of interest. I wrote a lot of notes after I invented Victor. I found that my popularity was directly proportional to how long and juicy my notes were.

2/12/83. Mini- How are you? How's Diego? I'm fine. I'm in Civics. José Castillo just squeezed José Urbino until he passed out. It was really funny. José U. drooled! Mr. Humphrey didn't even notice. I had such a great weekend. Victor and I went to Boca Raton and shopped all day Sunday. He bought me a cute little promise ring. It sucks because I can't wear it, or my mother will ask where it came from. I hate this. Every weekend I have to go to my cousin's if I want to see Victor. And of course I want to see him. My cousin's mom is so cool. She knows about Victor but doesn't tell my mom. I wish you could meet him. You will soon, I promise. ¡Qué pena! Humphrey just saw me. Gotta go. Write back.

I worked in the principal's office an hour a day. It was better than study hall, and I could get away with a lot. Monday, while I was doing some errands, I pulled Minita out of class. I told the teacher her mother was on the phone. We ran to the bathroom that was across from Sylvia's locker.

"I have to pee," she giggled and went into a stall.

"You got the note, right?"

"Yeah. It's in my purse. I'm scared, man. Maybe we shouldn't do this."

I stared at the stall door, waiting for her to say something else.

"You sure we won't get caught?"

"Minita, don't worry. Sylvia thinks we're her friends."

"OK," she said, coming out of the stall. "Let's go."

We checked the hall to see if it was clear, then tiptoed to the locker. Minita reached into her purse, pulled out a folded piece of paper, and handed it to me. I fed it into the locker vent.

"Well," sighed Minita, "we can't do anything about it now."

I walked with her back to class, then went back to the office. I started to feel a little squeamish. If we did get caught, we'd be in a lot of trouble.

I ran into Gloria after class.

"Hey, man. Why'd you take Minita out of class and not me?"

"I couldn't get you both out at the same time, OK?"

She smirked. Gloria and I had been close friends ever since grade school. But in eighth grade she had started working at Eckerd Drug, so she didn't have as much time to spend with me and Minita. Sometimes Gloria seemed to resent my close relationship with Minita.

"Shit, man. I wanted to get out so bad," she said. "I was so bored."

"Maybe next week."

"How's Victor?"

"He's fine. He got me a ring."

"Yeah, where is it?"

"I can't wear it. If my mother sees it, I'm dead."

"Your parents suck, man."

"See you later," I said, and escaped into my home economics classroom. Gloria made me nervous. She was less trusting and maybe smarter than Minita. I didn't like talking to her about Victor. She always looked a little suspicious. She had a lot more experience with guys than Minita did. She knew Cuban guys didn't go out with girls as homely as me. She was no prize herself. She had to sleep with her boyfriends if she wanted to keep them for any amount of time. Everybody knew that, but nobody really blamed her.

While I was cooking my omelette under the green fluorescents of the classroom, I decided that I was going to have to turn Victor into more of a louse, in order to make him believable.

It took two days for Sylvia to even find the note, her locker was such a mess. Minita and I were on edge every time there was a class change. Sylvia would babble on and on about the new pair of Jordache jeans she had just bought or her conflict about getting a perm. Minita and I exchanged knowing glances: this time she would find it.

Finally, she did—ironically enough, on Valentine's day.

Sylvia pulled the note out of her locker, and looked at it curiously. "So I told my mom, 'Look. I want a perm, OK? What's wrong with getting a perm? It's not like an ankle bracelet or something.'" She unfolded the note. "You know, because all the whores in Cuba wear ankle bracelets." She rolled her eyes, then looked down at the note. "Oh my God."

"What's wrong?" I asked. Minita made herself busy with her locker.

Sylvia looked at me with terrified eyes. I felt a twinge of remorse. Then she started to cry. What a wimp, I thought. She pushed the note in my face. I read it very slowly, faking disbelief. "C'mon," I said. "Let's go to the office." I put my arm around Sylvia and started guiding her down the hall. I looked over my shoulder to see Minita with a panic-stricken expression on her face. I gave her a reassuring nod, but she just shook her head.

"I can't believe you took her to the office," Minita said after school. We were in her backyard, sipping rum and cokes. We had replaced her parent's rum with water.

"That was the best thing I could do," I said. "Now they'll never suspect me."

"Yeah, but what about me?"

"How would they suspect you? Everybody loves you."

"That's not true."

"Well, they like you better than me."

"What? Dacia, where is this coming from?"

"Never mind."

We sat quietly for a minute. Her stupid dog kept tossing a mahoe leaf in the air with his mouth, trying to catch it.

"How's Victor?" she asked.

"He's good."

"Good, huh?" she laughed.

"I think I want to get on the pill," I said nonchalantly.

"*What*?"

"Well, we keep fooling around and getting so close..."

"Dacia, you're only fifteen."

"So?"

We stayed quiet. Her ice tinkled in the glass as she took a sip.

"When do I get to meet him?"

"Soon."

"Diego wants to double date."

"That's sounds fun," I said.

2/19/83. Mini— Everything is going so fast. Friday me and Victor went to Club 51. We danced all night. It was so much fun. He took me down to the Yacht Club later. We walked on the dock and then he says, "Well, here it is, El Soltero.*" So I say, "'The bachelor?' What a stupid name for a boat." And then he tells me that it's* his. *His father gave it to him for his sixteenth birthday. I freaked. We went down in the cabin and it's amazing. Mini, I'm in love. This place had a stocked bar and a shower—and this bed. Well, OK, so a lot happened. In fact, and if you tell anybody I'll kill you. Not even Gloria. I lost my virginity. Don't worry, we were careful. I liked it. Remember when we used to wonder what size it would be like (carrot or kosher dill)? DILL PICKLE all the way! But I get the feeling that he did it before—a lot. And he got up and took a shower almost as soon as he was done. Oh well, DESTROY THIS NOTE. There's the bell. I'll write later.*

The afternoon of that note, Minita came over, and we walked around the block for hours, talking about sex. I was lucky to have read plenty of explicit romance novels.

"What did it feel like?" Minita asked.

"Well, it hurt a little. But it felt pretty good."

"I can't believe he took a shower afterwards. What a jerk."

I shrugged.

We taunted the neighbor's chow-chow by pushing a stick at it through the holes in the fence. It growled at us.

"Do you think you love Victor?"

"I don't know. I guess so."

"I think I love Diego. He keeps asking me if I want to do it. I don't know. Maybe we will." She threw down her stick and started walking. "This thing with Sylvia went too far. She's got three girls walking her home every day."

I laughed. "It's been almost a week, and she still hasn't gotten over it?"

"Well, wouldn't you be scared?" Minita asked.

"I don't know. Probably not."

"Gloria said that she thinks you're the one who put the note in Sylvia's locker," Minita said, nearly whispering.

"She did?"

"I told her you didn't."

"Well, we don't really have anything to worry about, do we? She's not friends with Sylvia."

"Yeah, but watch out for her. I don't know. I don't think she likes you anymore."

"Is she working today?" I asked.

"I think it's her day off."

"Well, let's go pay her a visit."

Gloria lived two blocks away. She was part of one of those large Cuban families where the front door is constantly open. Halfway up the walk to her house, the strong smell of garlic practically knocked me out. We rapped on the open door before we went in, but no one could hear us over the sound of the Argentinian soap opera and Gloria's mother yelling. We walked in. "¡Guillermo! ¡Qué estupido! I told you to pick up your room a hundred times!"

"Hola," called Minita.

"Ay, niñas. I'm sorry. It's always the same thing around here. So much yelling." I'm sure she thought she was speaking in a normal tone, but she was still yelling, the TV was so loud. "Gloria's in her room."

Gloria was painting her toenails. The soap was also blaring on her little black and white TV.

"Pero, Sylvia is so scared you guys," she said.

"Who walked her home today?" asked Minita.

"Me and Lupe."

"I didn't know you were Sylvia's friend," I said.

"I feel sorry for her, man. She doesn't know if it's somebody from school or some crazy man on the street. She doesn't feel safe anywhere."

"Poor thing," I shook my head. I looked up. Gloria was looking at me, a trace of a smile on her lips. "Do you think she really has anything to worry about?"

"No," said Gloria, looking me straight in the eye, "I think some chick at school did it."

Minita flipped casually through a magazine. I felt her tensing up.

"Really?" I acted extremely interested. "Who do you think it is?"

"I don't know. But she's a good actress, whoever she is." Gloria screwed the cap onto her nail polish. She blew at her toes dramatically. "So," she said slowly. "How's Victor, Dacia?"

"He's doing great."

"Yeah? Did you go at it yet?"

"Gloria!" Minita looked up from her magazine, her eyes wide.

"C'mon, Minita. I know what rich guys are like. Don't try and tell me you didn't do it yet, Dacia. Because then I *really* won't believe you."

"Believe me about what?"

"Victor, of course. This guy is too good to be true, man." She turned to look at the TV. "Shit. Violeta is pregnant."

Minita looked at me anxiously. For the first time, I felt uncomfortable about inventing Victor. I thought about coming clean right there, telling them it had all been a joke. But I had gone too far already. I'd lose their respect completely if I told the truth.

"OK. Victor and I did it. Are you happy? It's my business, that's why I didn't tell you."

"Don't get pregnant," was all that Gloria said.

Gloria's mother peeked in the door and told her it was time for dinner. "Is Sylvia coming to eat?" she asked.

"Si, Mámi, her dad is dropping her off," Gloria said.

Minita raised her eyebrows at me.

"Póbrecita," said Gloria's mother. She shook her head, and closed the door behind her.

"Your mom knows?" Minita asked.

"Yeah, my mom has English class at night with Sylvia's mom. Her mother is really upset," Gloria said.

Gloria walked us to the open door. It was getting near dark. My father was probably going to kill me for leaving my block. Minita and I walked quietly, enjoying the cool evening air.

We stood and talked in front of Minita's house. "My mom knows Gloria's mom," she said. She looked frightened.

"So?"

"I don't want my mom hearing about this."

"Don't worry, man."

"Your mom knows Gloria's mom too. And your grandmother saw us making that note," her voice trembled.

INVENTING VICTOR

Weekends were the worst for me. I guess I had brought it upon myself. I couldn't leave the house for the fear that Minita would see me. I was supposed to be at my cousin's every weekend.

Saturday night I watched out the window as Diego came to pick up Minita. She looked cute in a little miniskirt. She hopped into his car. I saw her silhouette lean over to kiss him. It was a long kiss.

I wrote a long note to her about Victor, and dated it for Monday.

2/26/83 Mini— I'm so depressed. Victor and I got into a really bad fight. I went to my cousin's on Friday, and I was so excited because Victor said we had his parents' house all weekend. My cousin slept over her friend's house so her mother would think we were both over there.

It was great—at first. Victor made me Filet Mignon with a baked potato and baby carrots and we drank wine from the 1960s! Then he puts on some music and we start dancing. It was that song Europa *(you know, the one with the saxophone). And he dedicated the song to me. Then he tells me to turn my back to him and close my eyes. I heard him leave the room for a minute. Then he came back and put something warm and soft around my shoulders. He said, "Open your eyes." I opened them, and looked down, and I was wearing a beautiful black mink coat. I was a little drunk. I kissed him and thanked him and the next thing I knew, I was crying. I mean, it was so awful, because I would never be able to wear this coat. My parents would want to know where it came from, of course. And so, he said, "Don't worry, because we're going to go to New York next weekend. You can wear it there." And I said, "I can't go to New York. My aunt would never let me. She might tell my parents about you and then I won't be able to see you at all!" He got really mad. He told me that the reason my parents treat me like a baby is because I act like one, and that I should stick up for myself, and all this shit. He was yelling so loud. I said I would try to think of a way that I could go to New York. I would try to make up a lie. And then he called me a liar. He said I wasn't honest with anybody. And then he said that I probably lie to him too. He accused me of cheating on him! He said, "You're probably lying about your parents. They probably let you go out with ten different guys in a week. You just lie to me so you can screw me on the weekends and screw other guys during the week."*

Minita, I couldn't believe he was saying this to me. I said, "You're so paranoid. You're crazy." And he said, "Oh, yeah? You have to have practice to screw like such a slut. Where did you get your practice?"

I threw the coat down on the ground and I reached for the closest possible thing to throw at him—which just happened to be this incredibly valuable antique vase from Spain. You should have seen the look on his face. It was kind of funny. The vase went whizzing by his head and hit the wall behind him. It shattered into a million pieces. He completely freaked. He started running around in little circles and yelling, "That is irreplaceable, you bitch! ¡Puta! ¡Puta!" He was babbling in Spanish like crazy. I could hardly understand him. Then he came over to me and slapped me hard across the face. He hit me so hard that I fell. I got up and slapped him back, of course. He went over to the table and swigged from the wine bottle. He paced the room awhile and then said, "I'm taking you home." He didn't say a word to me the entire ride. He took me to my cousin's friend's house. Luckily, they were asleep, because my face looked really bad. I put on so much makeup the next morning. Mini, I'm so upset. I want to go to New York. I don't know where this fight came from. I hope he calls me at my cousin's house next weekend. Well, sorry to depress you. Write back.

I wrote a note to Gloria that was almost an exact duplicate. My mother came in the room. "What are you writing?" she asked in Spanish.

"A story."

"Mmm. About what?"

"A girl."

She nodded and sat down on the bed with me. I closed my notebook. "I heard about that girl at your school who is being chased by some loco. Do you know her?"

"Yes. Sylvia. She only got one note from him. I don't think he's chasing her."

"Well, your father wants you to come home right after school. You stop going to Minita's. She can come here. And don't walk around the block anymore."

"Mámi! Because one girl gets one stupid note, I'm a prisoner in the house now?"

"The note was sick, Dacia. It was made of letters cut up from a magazine." I heard a gasp from my doorway, and turned to see my grandmother standing there, listening. She walked into the room. Her hands fluttered around her neck. She started yelling. "Show your mother your magazines!" She left the room, waving her hands in the air.

"What is she talking about?" my mother asked, alarmed.

"She's a crazy old lady," I said. My heart thumped.

My mother went to my desk and pulled magazines from it, flipping through them. I thanked God that I had thrown out the ones Minita and I had used. She threw the last magazine down, and looked at me. "If I find out that you have anything to do with this, young lady, you won't be able to go out into the front yard."

"Oh, big difference. What a threat!" I yelled after her. She pulled the door firmly behind her.

On Monday morning, I made up my face to look like I had a bruise. I dashed past my grandmother, out of the house before she could get a good look at me. Minita hopped into the bus that picked us up for school. She looked at me and gasped.

"What happened?" she whispered. "Did you get in trouble with your dad?"

"No," I said. "Read this." I handed her the note.

"Oh my God. You poor thing," she said as we got off the bus. She was gazing at me with admiration. "He's so terrible to you. But, you know, it's so romantic. Diego and I fight over what movie to see. You *live* a movie."

At lunch, Gloria sat with us, and we discussed what I should do about Victor. Gloria said I should break up with him, but Minita thought I should give him another chance. It became pretty apparent that the worse Victor treated me, the more they liked the relationship, the more interesting it was. Gloria seemed to believe it, too.

I continued writing more elaborate notes. Victor left me on the side of the road in the middle of nowhere, and I had to take a cab back to my cousin's house. I caught Victor at a club feeling up another girl. Victor took me to New York, bought me a diamond bracelet, then later tried to strangle me in the hotel room because he thought I was flirting with the bellhop. Sometimes I broke up with him, for a week or two, but we always got back together, and usually he bought me something valuable to celebrate our reconciliation.

Unfortunately, the more interesting my notes got, the more they wanted to meet him. Minita even suggested that she go with me to my cousin's for a weekend. I made up an excuse about there not being enough room at my cousin's house; I didn't want to upset my aunt by loading too much company on her.

Once I came to school faking excitement. I told Gloria and Minita that Victor was driving all the way from his house on Miami Beach to visit me at school. After school let out, we waited out in the parking lot for an hour. I kept saying how he was always late, he would come eventually, and then I started to cry. The tears came surprisingly easy. They comforted me and seemed to believe me completely.

A strange thing started happening with Minita. She and Diego began fighting constantly. She said she didn't know how it started, but they were always yelling at each other, fighting over stupid things.

One day we were sitting on my porch, where I was basically trapped, and she talked about her latest tiff with Diego.

"He wanted to buy me something for our anniversary, he said, so when I picked out this little tiny promise ring, he said, 'Oh, that's too much money.' I mean, Dacia, I don't care if he gets me anything. It's just that, he's so cheap. I'd rather have something nice than a cheap little charm. He wants to get me one of those awful 'taken' charms. God, and *you* get mink coats." She laughed and sipped at her Coke.

"Yeah, but I screw Victor."

At the time, I vaguely knew that it was my fault. She was fighting with Diego about promise rings because she wanted a Victor. She even seemed to want the violence.

"We got into this big fight and he called me a spoiled brat, so I slapped him across the face," she said.

"Did he slap you back?"

"Yes." She held her hand up to her face.

"Minita! That's terrible."

"What? Victor slaps *you* all the time."

"Yeah, but it's different."

"Why?"

"Because," I said.

She stared blankly at me.

"Because I screw Victor."

Minita started having sex with Diego. She said she liked it. But it didn't seem to help their relationship. Friday and Saturday nights started getting noisy around our neighborhood. Diego would drop her off at eleven, they would stand out in the driveway and argue, her mother would come out and yell in Spanish, then he would drive off, his tires squealing.

I decided to plan a trip to Paris for myself and Victor. We would fly there, spend one glorious evening, then have a glorious fight, and come back broken up for good. I didn't like what my relationship with Victor was doing to Minita and Diego.

"I'm going to Lake Placid this weekend," said Minita at lunch one day. "This sucks. I hate fishing. And my parents won't let me stay home. They won't let Diego go with us either. My mother thinks I need time away from him."

"That's OK," said Gloria. "I have to go to a retreat. A bunch of relatives telling you what sinners they are. My fingers are gonna hurt from doing the rosary, man."

"You gonna tell them how many guys you been with, Gloria?" I asked.

"Hey, at least the guys I been with don't beat me," she laughed.

"Yeah, well they don't take you to Paris either," Minita said.

"Paris?" asked Gloria.

I nodded.

"You're going this weekend?"

"He can afford it," I said, and laughed.

"How long you been with Victor?"

"Two months."

"And he's taking you to Paris? I mean, OK, he's rich right? But, God." she scraped the cheese off her pizza and started eating the crust. "Hey, didn't you say that he goes to Belen Prep?"

"No, I said St. Brendan's." I *had* said Belen, but I suspected that she had been checking up.

"Oh, OK, because I know somebody from Belen who says he never heard of Victor Puentes."

"Victor goes to St. Brendan's."

"OK. Don't get bitchy, man. One private school is as good as the other." She smiled. She held the stringy cheese over her mouth and gulped it down.

Gloria was difficult to read. One minute she seemed completely convinced, even fascinated, by my stories about Victor, and the next minute, she was checking up on me, suspicious as ever.

"How's Sylvia?" Minita asked Gloria.

"She's all right. She's pretty cool. We went skating last Friday. She's really good at it."

"Does she walk home alone yet?" I asked.

"No, she's still nervous, man."

"It's been like two months," said Minita.

"I never thought she would take it so hard," I said.

I don't know how it popped out like that. It was the first real mistake I had made. Gloria looked up at me, slowly.

"I mean," I said, "when she got the note, sure, she should be upset, but to keep being scared for months, that's taking it hard, man."

"Yeah, taking it hard," said Gloria, smiling. "Hey, aren't you the one who took her to the office the day she found the note?"

"Yeah."

"That was real nice of you, Dacia. Sylvia says she doesn't know what she would have done without you there." She nodded her head slowly at me, and kept smiling that creepy smile.

I looked at Minita. She sucked on her straw intently and stared at a spot on the table. I felt dizzy. I went to the bathroom and hung over the toilet for awhile, but I couldn't throw up.

I tried to run inside when Diego drove into Minita's driveway that Saturday, but my grandmother had locked the front door. I couldn't get in. I started to go around to the side door, but when I looked across the street he was already waving to us. My mother waved back enthusiastically. I hoped he hadn't seen me, but I was pretty sure he had.

I went to my room. I couldn't believe that I had forgotten about Minita's dog. Of course somebody had to feed her dog while she was away.

I started concocting a note about Victor standing me up, going to a quínce instead of taking me to Europe, the louse. But I was tired. I fell asleep instead.

There it was in front of me when I woke.

Mini—Victor and me are over finally. How could he go to his cousin's quínce when we were supposed to go to Paris?

It sounded so fake. I realized that I was getting bad at this. I wished I had never started it. Everything seemed to be caving in, just when I was going to stop it anyway. I wished it hadn't gone so far.

"I know why you're like this," said Gloria.

I looked at Minita, wishing she would defend me.

"Your life is so boring, man. You can't even go out of your yard. That's why you make up a rich boyfriend who punches you in the nose once a week. That's why you put a rape note in Sylvia's locker. She never even did anything to you."

I widened my eyes.

"I know you did it. Minita told me, man."

I looked back at Minita, but she would not look up.

"You think you're giving us a dose of *reality*, right? But it's just bullshit. 'Bullshit,' by Dacia."

"OK," said Minita. She looked straight at Gloria, didn't once look at me. "So, it was bullshit. But, you didn't even believe Victor existed until they slept together. And you believed it even more when they started to fight."

"Yeah, I know it was well-written bullshit." She turned and looked at me. "But man, we can do without it. Ask Minita here. Ask her about reality." She got up and picked up her tray. "And don't lie to your friends." Gloria walked away.

Minita sat staring at her fork-spoon. I was quiet for awhile, waiting for her to say something. Finally, I couldn't stand it anymore.

"What was she talking about? What am I supposed to ask you?" I asked.

She sighed. She pushed her hand through her hair and didn't look at me. "I'm pregnant," she groaned.

A lump formed in my throat. "You are?"

"I went to the clinic this morning. That's why I was late for school. Me and Diego—we were very stupid." She continued looking down.

"We were all stupid," I said.

"Not Gloria. She wasn't stupid. She never believed you. I believed you all along. And then I tried to be like you. I was mean to Diego just because he was nice to me. I wanted to have dramatic fights like you did, passionate sex like you did. I was the stupidest of all of us." She looked up at me with tears in her eyes.

"I'm sorry," I said.

She shook her head. "Why did you do it, Dacia?"

"I don't know. I guess I just wanted to be like you. To have a boyfriend. To have some excitement in my life."

"You know," she said, "now I wish I'd never had any excitement at all."

"I'm here to help you, Mini. Whatever you do. Whatever you decide."

"Yeah, okay," she said, standing to go. And I knew my offer was pathetic, that no one had any reason to trust in me, or depend on me.

After school, I looked all over for Sylvia Hernandez. Finally I saw her walking alone on the bridge over the canal. I caught up with her and asked if I could explain a few things. I told her how I had put the note in her locker. I didn't say anything about Minita's involvement. Sylvia didn't interrupt.

We walked under the highway overpass and up the catwalk. When I was finished, she stopped walking and turned toward me. We stood at the top of the catwalk looking at each other, surrounded by chain-link, cars zipping under us at a dizzying rate. For the first time, I noticed that her eyes were a very pretty green.

"Are you done?" she asked.

"I think you should kick my ass," I said, and I meant it.

She raised her chin slightly. "Why don't you ask your imaginary boyfriend to kick your ass?"

I didn't say anything as Sylvia walked away in her tight Jordache jeans. I turned toward the fence, staring out over the cars. A red Porsche squealed onto the highway and I thought of Victor. I knew I would miss him. I wished I could go to Minita's house, tell her all about Victor and what had happened with Sylvia, as if it were a funny story that had occurred while she was away on summer vacation. But it wasn't a very funny story. And she hadn't been away; she'd been more involved than I had ever intended.

I yearned for the relief that would have come if only Sylvia had thrown that punch, if only she had restored the dramatic balance. But such resolutions only happened in Victor's world, and I didn't live there anymore.

The Details of Women

JENNIFER BANNAN

At the WalMart where she's shopped for years, my wife Allison is picking up another ornamental flag. There in the Patio Center she meets a woman and they get to talking. They finish shopping and go to a coffee house and then Allison remembers her ice cream is melting. But they're really hitting it off, so Allison invites the woman over to our house to continue the chat over our kitchen table.

By the time I get home, they've discovered just how much they have in common, because this woman is Rebecca Flint, my ex-girlfriend from twenty-four years ago. It's Rebecca, now Rebecca Weiss, who I lived with in Paris during the student protests. She is the woman who managed to destroy what taste I had for risk and worldliness and she is here, sitting in my kitchen.

She and Allison have been laughing and Rebecca has that slumped posture she always had when she laughed, like it causes her pain, but it's a pain she wouldn't give up. There is no difference but a few, few hairline wrinkles. She is beautiful still. She must have made some serious changes soon after we ended the relationship. No way she could have kept her looks with the life she was leading when I last saw her.

Her life is, from the sound of it, a lot like mine, with the two kids in high school and the husband Bernie at the law firm and the Tudor with oddly shaped rooms and drafty windows, and she tells me all of this with no irony whatsoever.

So, now that I'm over the shock, I ask, Hey, when I walked in, what was so funny? I want to know, and Allison gets up and begins putting cans in the cupboard, her large body juxtaposed next to the still, straight lines of Rebecca in her chair, who looks at me with that expression I can't read: Urgency? Playfulness? Regret? and says how it's just strange that of all places to move that she and her husband could have ended up here in Morgantown. They've been here for two years, she explains.

But *that's* not very funny. Strange and a little creepy, yes, but not that funny. They were laughing, and I think they were laughing about me.

I was covering political unrest and student riots for the wire. Rebecca was photographing the same. We kept running into each other at the rallies, at the newspaper taverns later. We were just out of college ourselves and felt awkward covering events that, by virtue of our age, we could have been involved in. So we told ourselves documenting the events was an important and powerful thing.

Rebecca was intense. She would choke on teargas for a good photograph, while my time there involved lengthy conversations with top dignitaries, in their warm studies with cigar smoke filling the room. I was first to know the details of how many arrested, how many injured, but they were details I rarely witnessed myself. I talked to the students, but usually they presented their spokesperson: the over-mature, diplomatic counterpart who represented the philosophy, not the action. I was no Rebecca, up to her ears in the fury of the protestors.

I remember the afternoon when she burst into my one-room apartment with the most disturbing of her often surprising exclamations: “I threw a homemade bomb.” Her eyes were glittering and it was only two long strides from my desk to hold her where she stood at the door. “They handed it to me and I threw it!”

I don’t think she realized the gravity of what had happened to her until she was in my arms. When I first held her, she was laughing, but within minutes she was sobbing.

I felt her skin buzz under my fingertips and I knew that the hesitancy that kept us just friends was about to dissolve. “I sympathize with them,” she said. “But it’s not our battle, is it?”

Finally we were holding each other in the way I had most wanted us to, and she wasn’t pulling away. She looked up at me and I saw the spark of decision in her eyes, the same I had seen before, whenever she chose to do something impulsive or daring. From then on she had me.

When I returned home from Paris, no girlfriend, no courage, I asked to be put on the business desk. I figured, streams of press releases from corporations. Careful words about executives being pushed out and fresh, hungry ones ready to take charge. Natural stuff, nothing revolutionary. But— the heated discussions before a big story broke, the hum at my toes from the presses below— newspaper life made me anxious. It made me want to be a part of the important stuff. And since my nerve had dried up, I wanted out altogether.

A friend told me that people were making money in computers and I took a class, then quit work and got a degree in programming, followed by a job that paid twice my newspaper salary.

I met Allison at the college bookstore. She had been a student but hated it and quit classes, keeping her job. I liked the way Allison could laugh about her failure at college, could stay and work at the bookstore when anyone else would have taken a job elsewhere or at least taken on a rebellious air. We dated on the weekends and on the day I was offered a job I stopped by the bookstore and asked her to marry me. She said she'd think about it and would call me after her shift was over. Nothing reckless there—nothing difficult either. I walked around our small town with its boring shops, easy with the lack of activity or strife, fully expecting the "yes" that Allison would give me that evening.

Sometimes my software crashes, like now. I jot down an error message and reboot. The computer taps and sighs and slowly works itself into motion. I pick up the blue stress ball and wait. My screen opens and up comes a picture of my family—Allison, Felicia and me, in front of our house, a suburban house with the hedges and green shutters and the decorative flag Felicia criticizes when she's home from college. Allison ignores Felicia and changes this flag every month: poinsettia in December, chickadee and snowflakes in February, and in August, watermelon slices with bites taken from them.

"Hey, we thought we'd stop by," Allison says. She's standing here, at my office, with Rebecca beside her. They've been seeing each other all the time now. And for the first time in my marriage, I don't trust Allison. What has Rebecca said during their chats and why is Allison so eager to hear it? I look at Rebecca and I feel a strange stirring I didn't know could be awakened.

"Look at that," Rebecca says to Allison. "Staring at a picture of his ladies all day. What a family man!"

"I'm rebooting," I say, but it means nothing to them.

"A cube, huh?" Rebecca says. She tilts her head to tell me she's kidding, but I can't help the heat in my neck.

"Everybody has cubicles here. It's a flat organization. Some kind of new business model. The CEO has a cube!" I set down the stress ball and stretch widely, illustrating the roominess of my workspace— I'm probably coming off as defensive.

"OK, sweetie," says Allison. "We just wanted to let you know that we're going to be out for the night. There's an art festival in Wheeling. It goes till 10 p.m., so we thought we'd just get a hotel and come back in the morning."

"What about Felicia?" Our daughter is still home from college, on spring break, until Sunday. Her presence in the house disturbs me. She mumbles in disdain about the stifling suburban environment, the ridiculous people, the ridiculous homes. Part of me agrees with her but I don't know of a solution and so far she hasn't offered one either.

"Felicia will be fine!" Allison says, rolling her eyes in exasperation. Her comfort with bickering in front of Rebecca is intensely irritating to me.

Rebecca asks me if there's a women's room around anywhere, trying to give me a minute alone with Allison. It's terrifying to me that my ex of twenty-four years understands the need for decorum, while my spouse doesn't.

Allison was never smart. I married her with that knowledge. She has been fun and easy instead. She has been a good mother to our daughter and a good wife to me. When I touch her I think of the summer days at Lake Erie, sand stuck to wet skin—Felicia's, Allison's, mine—the skin of family. I love Allison for many things, but mainly the comfort she has provided our little group.

"What are you doing?" I ask, when Rebecca is a safe distance away.

"What do you mean?" Allison has the habit of opening her eyes in the most artificially childish way. But this is so unlike her, to make things difficult.

"Why does she have to be your new best friend?"

"Mark, what's the big deal?"

"You don't have anything in common," I say.

"I disagree. Rebecca's a lot of fun."

"She's using you."

"For what?" Allison pulls her arm away from me.

"For some sick illusion about her past."

"I think she likes me. And I think you're rude. We're not interested in talking about you, if that's your concern, Mr. Self-absorbed."

"Please think about how this makes me feel. Rebecca and I finished on very bad terms. It was a very *complicated* time in my life. I have trouble seeing her again and again." I'm gripping her arm again. If she won't hear me now, I decide, then she must not care.

She says gently, "I haven't made that many friends since Felicia has gone off to school, Mark. I know it's a strange coincidence, but I'm enjoying myself."

Rebecca appears again at my cube. I swear there is some glee in her eye, seeing me and Allison this close up, this intense. Rebecca knows their friendship tortures me.

"Like fractals," Felicia says, as, on the drive back to her campus in Harrisburg, we pass Three Mile Island. It's a moment to note, because she never says anything. She's just this sullen limp rag all the time. I swear she looks strung out; sometimes she reminds me of Rebecca during the Paris days.

"What do you mean fractals, honey?" Allison says, looking at the reactors. Her hands twist in her lap and they are the hands of a middle-aged woman.

"Yes, what do you mean?" Rebecca asks, and that's the stinking truth: Rebecca is with us on this drive. Allison convinced her to go at the last minute. They thought it would be fun to drag me to the outlet malls after dropping off Felicia.

"Fractals are shapes in nature that repeat themselves. And those reactors are the shape that man created when he first chopped down a tree."

"Oh," I get it and look over at Allison to see if she does too, but I can't tell. "They are shaped something like tree stumps. Pretty tall tree stumps."

It's funny, looking at the white stumps on the banks of the Susquehanna, to imagine the giants swinging their giant axes through the air, clearing their patch, making room for their big elbows and knees and creating a place to sit. Big, pale stumps and ashen giants wearily resting on them.

"You're a perceptive young woman," Rebecca is saying. And I remember shoving my hands down Rebecca's capri pants on the bank of the Seine, loving it when she slapped me and wriggled away. How she chirped in that new French accent of hers, and how the old men looked over and laughed in their stubbly-chin way.

"You like the energy of our young people?" one of those men asked us on a spring day much like this one. "It excites you because young people in America are becoming calm again."

"There's plenty of youth movement in the States," Rebecca argued. She was taller than the Frenchman, which somehow seemed rude. I wished the conversation would end.

"We are all like this in France: revolutionaries in our youth. Then at age thirty we join the bourgeoisie. All of us. It's a national joke. It may be special to America, but it's nothing to us!"

I drive and remember that man, knowing it's true all over the Western world. There are few fights we can sustain, so we beat the energy out of ourselves. If we aren't born beaten then we beat ourselves down.

Felicia will do it. She'll repeat our mistakes, whether with drugs, like Rebecca, or fear, like me. We're fractals, shapes repeating ourselves.

Now Felicia is safely behind us at school; the clammy feel of her cheek, reluctant as ever, lingers on my lips. My wife and Rebecca drag me to the Linens n Things outlet shop and force me to evaluate towels and sheets. I find it grotesquely ironic, Rebecca handling these intimate items as though it's nothing to her that I am here. She throws a massive towel around herself and traipses about the aisles of the store, raving to Allison that it really is the perfect size.

I remember her dripping wet from the tub in my apartment, which she loved because it was in the open space next to the kitchen, no walls or partitions. I used to give her plates of eggs there while she bathed. This was before the drugs. Her eyes were bright then and sometimes I would sit at my typewriter and work and catch her setting aside her eggs to grab the camera, the water in the tub sloshing—and she'd take picture after picture of me, of the room. I wonder if she still has those photos.

The window behind her head in those days let in the kind of yellow light that made the dirty dishes in the sink look subversive and sexy. In the distance was the river in its broken glass sparkle and sometimes we'd hear the rising chants of students and put on our clothes and go out to see what was happening.

Her hair was a tumble. A mane. She wore those capri pants all the time, which were out of fashion in the States, where everything was loose and wide. But in Paris those pants were perfect, she was a little nymph, a cat who would spring away, I could feel it, even then I knew I would lose her.

Does she remember? Because I do. I remember holding her on the braided rug next to the tub and the rug was wet the way hair in the tub drain is wet and matted, threatening to pull you down.

She wasn't there. Her cold thin body was there, but her eyes were floating back white in her head. I rocked her and couldn't find a pulse and I had been at the newspaper and had just turned in my story and my boss had told me that he was entering it for a prestigious award.

So, I was ready to tell her my good news. I knew she had been doing drugs but I didn't think it was so bad. But then I walked into the apartment and she was blue in the water.

So I had to do something with the dead girl. I picked her up. I was clumsy, maybe a little rough. I went to the phone but then suddenly she was moaning and breathing and I was shaking her and yelling at her for dying.

A month or so after Linens n Things, I come home from work and they are cozied up on the bed in white, plush robes, painting each other's toenails.

"We're having spa day!" Rebecca announces proudly. Her towel slips from its turban and her dark hair snakes around her robe's collar with slow-motion grace.

"Oops."

It should have been me to tell Allison the details. The bathtub, the chants from the students outside, the death scare. But, they're bathing together, here in the safe house where overdoses and love affairs are nothing but titillating fictions. They must have talked about it. They must have discussed the bathtub in my old flat. I can just imagine how Rebecca paints a picture of me: the scared lover who lost his nerve for the real world.

I suppose it's surprising I never talked to Allison about my time in Paris. But I wanted to forget. I didn't think they were memories I savored—until now, when I feel they're being robbed from me by the same person who so dramatically created them. The same person whose hip rises before me under a white terry cloth robe. She's beautiful and it's not fair that she's on my bed.

"I was hoping to get a nap. I have a splitting headache." I say.

Rebecca opens polish remover and pours it onto a cotton ball.

"God, that stuff stinks," I say, surprising myself with the contempt in my voice.

"Felicia's room is very comfortable in the late afternoon," Allison says, concentrating on Rebecca's pinky toe, unfazed by my tone. "The lighting is just right for a nap."

"Nothing's sacred with you two, is it?" I start to shout.

They both stare at me blankly. I leave the house. I drive around. I don't know where to go. There is nowhere to go.

The drive-thru at Kentucky Fried Chicken reminds me of a prison. I imagine the people inside are serving a sentence, they can only reach out the window for brief, superficial contact with others.

I eat the sandwich in three bites, lick my hands like an animal. She can't trap me like this.

Many months later, Allison throws a barbecue on Memorial Day and Bernie and Rebecca come. Bernie is slick like a salamander. He says "IPO" three times within the first five minutes of his arrival. About an hour later, "aggregate" is the new word of choice.

They have a teenager who comes too, with three nose rings, which keep knocking into her hotdog bun when she eats. I think of the little processed pig that is her meal–did it have a nose ring too?

Rebecca has her camera, and she's making a big deal out of taking pictures of all the guests. I can't relate to my friends today and find myself bustling around to avoid talking to anyone. Some are from my office and they stand in slumped-shoulder huddles talking programming. They try to be snide and superior, to ridicule each other about operating system preferences, like the younger programmers in the office do — but they can't pull it off. They are still, like me, overwhelmed and a bit impressed by information technology. There's always so much more to learn.

Others here are from as far back as college, friends of Allison's from the bookstore, friends of mine from classes. Laughter spills from their little groups at the patio tables, at the dip table, under the oak tree, where Joe Hatfield flips over the hammock and loses his drink. He's up and laughing at himself, brushing grass from his thighs, slightly embarrassed. They're all nice enough, our friends. Nice, harmless, boring.

"Weird your ex-girlfriend lives here now," my friend Stan says, as I busy myself putting a new trash bag into the can.

"How'd you know that's who she is?"

"Oh, she's pretty proud of the story. Paris. Student riots. Heroin addiction. You wrote for the wire. I never knew that."

I shrug. Rebecca will tell everyone. There will be assumptions made about my character, about the person who chooses a docile life. I was fine – everybody was fine — with my life before she got here. I did not want to evaluate anything. My throat tightens, just like a little girl about to cry.

At least Allison is lovable today. She edges up to me frequently to kiss my cheek and straighten my apron. "I have something for you," she whispers in my ear while I'm manning the grill. She presses her large breast against my arm.

"What's that, honey?" I ask.

"Oh, you'll see."

Later when I'm laying out some hamburgers on the patio table, she yanks me by the apron strings and drags me around to the side of the house.

I like it because for once it's not about Rebecca. I don't know if it's because Bernie is here to keep Rebecca occupied, but Allison is more her old self. Not that person obsessed with Rebecca.

She stops me by the hedge and grabs the back of my head, pulls our faces together and gives me a deep tongue kiss.

"You little slut," I say, taking a handful of her big ass.

"That's all. I was watching you handle those wieners and I thought you looked hot. So I wanted to give you a sloppy kiss."

"I think I deserve more," I say and kiss her again.

She throws a large leg around mine. In my life I've been convinced to like bigness for the warm feel of it. My hard-on affirms this.

"The thrill is still there!" Rebecca calls out and we look up to see her at the back corner of the house, snapping our picture.

Allison laughs uproariously and I look at her, still gripping me, throwing her head back. She doesn't seem at all surprised that Rebecca has appeared. I feel the oddest sensation of a set-up.

I want to be a good sport, so when I push Allison away I do it gently, trying to chuckle. As I pass Rebecca on the way back to the backyard, I use every ounce of willpower to resist grabbing the camera out of her hand and hurling it out of the yard.

Two weeks later the picture is in the mailbox. Allison puts in on the refrigerator. It's up there for two days. One night I'm getting some milk at about 2 a.m. and I look at it for a long time. My face, surprised, almost scared, fills me with self-hatred. I don't know what it is I can't accept, but I want somehow to tell everyone that man is not me.

Allison looks like a doughy school lunch lady—-jolly, her hands in their casual contortions on my shoulders, her hair curling in sweaty tendrils around her wide face. Her leg is frozen in that unlikely raised position around me—like a flesh bumper protecting my pansy ass.

The grass behind us is brilliantly green; the hedge looks almost artificial. And worst of all, the flag that Allison hung at the front corner of the house, blowing in the breeze, a big springtime tulip and butterfly scene. Felicia hates these flags. She keeps threatening to hold a suburban-flag-burning.

Oh, the photo makes me want to die. I want to die looking at it. Finally I put the glass of milk down and I tear the photo off the fridge and I rip it into tiny pieces and I know this will upset Allison, but it's better than me dying so I think she'll understand.

The next day, after work, I see in the office parking lot a little wooden spoon from a kid's Italian ice on the ground and I think, "Fractals." But for what repeating pattern?

Then I realize that the pattern in that wooden spoon is nothing but the pattern of a spoon. Sometimes a spoon is just a spoon.

It's like knowing what you have to do. Knowing the pattern. Knowing you cannot let the pattern continue to repeat itself.

I get in my car and sit there with my hands against the hot wheel and I think about how Allison and Rebecca have been carrying on for months. Cuckolding me. Laughing about what a silly goose I was and have always been. I can't blame Allison because I've taken her for granted over the years. I feel she may deserve to torture me.

But Rebecca. She's tortured me once and she doesn't deserve another chance. So, I take the car to her house. I stand there ringing the bell, looking at her suburban flag, this one with a house on it. I guess this is her way of telling herself she really belongs in this neighborhood. But why an image of a house in front of house?

"I was wondering when you were finally going to come by," she says. She and Bernie have invited us to many barbecues, which Allison attends but I do not. "Well, come in. Take the Grand Tour," she says, and I walk behind her and see that she's wearing capri pants that I swear could be the same pants of twenty-four years ago. Her ass is high and shaped like a peach, really one of the best asses I've ever seen.

She walks me through the living room with the pitched ceiling and hearth as big as a stage. Down the hall, past many doors, she leads me into a bright study where her work is displayed on the wall: close up shots of flowers and birds and some interiors she's done for Better Homes and Gardens and Southern Living. "The dark room's in the basement," she says.

"I didn't really come for the tour. I came to talk," I say.

She's leaning on her desk, her hips tilted out slightly. She's looking around the walls at all the photos. "I'm sure you're wondering where all the shots are from *those* days," she says. "And I have them all. But you know, these mean just as much to me now. I think they're more what I'm about."

We should start over, I realize. She has mentioned the past now and I'm relieved at the possibility that we could reminisce about the two kids we were and not feel like we are talking about strangers. "I guess I haven't been fair," I say. "It's been hard to get to know you again because you're so close to Allison. And the past really looms, you know?" I smile, wanting her to know that I think some of the past was good.

"The past was complicated. I'm much more suited to this life," she nods. She straightens some things on her desk.

It isn't going as I'd hoped.

"I agree. I don't want to be reminded about the past. I want to *rebuke* the past." I am trying to sound firm but it's all wrong. Desperate instead.

"Well, sorry about that scary stuff, Mark," she says. "I really am. It scared me too."

We stand there and I think for a minute she will come over and touch me, but then I realize that she doesn't want that.

I don't know what she wants.

"Do you want forgiveness?" I ask.

"What are you talking about?"

"For the overdose."

"I did say I was sorry, but I guess I didn't think I was *looking* for forgiveness. I'm glad to be alive," she smiles and I see some pain there.

"Is there any way you'll leave Allison alone?" I ask.

"Allison is my friend. She's a much better person than either of us."

"That's easy to say about someone you don't respect."

"That's so ugly. Don't make assumptions about my respect level for Allison. Not based on yours."

"You're both just smitten with the big coincidence and you can't get over it long enough to see that you're completely different people," I say.

"We're long past the big coincidence. We don't *talk* about you. We agreed that it would be inappropriate."

"You ruined my taste for excitement and passion!" I'm suddenly screaming these over-the-top things and I know I should be embarrassed by myself, but I want her to know I feel this way. "Now you're Average Joe yourself, so what was the point of ruining it for me?"

She cocks her head. "You've lived without excitement or passion for twenty-four years?"

"You should be dead. Your life-style was supposed to kill you. But here you are! You can just jump into any life and call it your own."

"I'm comfortable in this life," she shrugs. "You're the one who seems to be having trouble, who seems to think he's sacrificed everything. Why don't you quit this martyr game and live a little? Go back into reporting."

"I have been satisfied with my life. Paris was forgotten. But day in, day out, you and Allison force me to remember," I say.

She shrugs again. She looks sad. Part of me wants to grip the sides of her face and kiss her until the girl I knew is standing before me.

"I remember when you left Paris," she says. "I saw you at the wire office and you had all of your things. I think I knew then how much you were hurting."

"I could have sworn you were strung out," I say.

"I was. But I remember you that day. You were pretty sad. You seemed like you'd had it. I felt bad. But I never thought it was all because of me. I'm still not sure it is."

She turns from me and straightens one of her photos on the wall.

I can't believe those photos—the flowers and interiors. I can't believe how things change.

"I was stupid," Rebecca continues. "But I hope you'll let me be friends with your wife. I love Allison."

There is a part of my little suburban area that reminds me of Paris. It is a street with small shops that has somehow been spared even one backlit plastic sign for McDonald's or Eckerd Drugs. The signs are carved wood, some hanging from iron chains and squeaking in the wind. I have seen people standing on the little bridge made of stone, with its gentle arch, as I am standing here now for the first time, looking into the shallow stream weaving into the low brambles. On the other side of the bridge there is a high school up the hill that could pass as a French governmental building. I stand on that bridge and look straight ahead, and imagine that there is a large city park behind the governmental building, that the shops have streets behind them with more shops continuing and continuing, and that the women coming out of the shops are speaking French, their heels clicking down the pavement.

It is all the same everywhere. There are shops and streams and stone and buildings and the details of women that break my heart.

So, when I return home I have made a decision. There is only one thing about this suburban life that is too, too much. I park the car and see that Allison is home. She won't like what I'm going to do so I simply do it.

I walk around the side of the house where the hedge is and climb onto the shoulders of the stone frog ornament so I can reach the flag in its tulip glory.

Around the rear of the house I head toward the grill, which I've been meaning to clean anyway. I rip off the lid like a chef and throw the flag on the metal grid. But stuck here in the corner is all wrong so I wheel the grill out to middle of the yard.

Allison opens the back door, asking, "Did you get steaks?"

"Oh!" She exclaims and comes down the porch steps to see what this is all about.

I've used a little lighter fluid by now. And I drop the match just as Allison realizes it's her flag that will cook.

"This flag means nothing, Allison. And that's the only thing I want gone from my life. Meaninglessness."

"It stands for spring," she says carefully.

"Spring doesn't need anything to stand for it. You should tell that to all of your friends."

She will understand me. Allison is real. She is genuine. She has to understand me.

I'm pushing with a stick at the burning flag, which melts and glows instead of creating flames, in the way only a really evil thing can melt, oily and cringing into itself. I steal a look at Allison and she is contemplative. Or perhaps mesmerized by the bluish blob that writhes and caresses itself.

"Felicia will be crushed she wasn't here for this," Allison says, shaking her head. "Here," she says, holding out her hand.

I give her the stick and she pushes at the flag to let the oxygen catch it, to create fresh sparks.

B and B

JENNIFER BANNAN

Because Catherine and John were liberals living in Pittsburgh, a segregated town with known race problems, they were committed to living in one of the few racially mixed neighborhoods. Their pride in this decision became a subtext of their lives.

But in sharp contrast to that pride was their disappointment at failing to befriend blacks in their neighborhood, despite their efforts. Among the things that hadn't worked were: joining the (mostly white) neighborhood board, volunteering at the local elementary school, and greeting their neighbors who passed them on the sidewalk with an open-ended question like "Got some good plans this weekend?"

They seemed to have very little in common with the blacks in the neighborhood, who rented instead of owned, who walked or took the bus instead of drove, who often mentioned the Lord in the brief discussions they had. John had been building a rapport with a school-aged girl over the course of one spring, but one day when he asked her to pick up the bag of Doritos she'd let flutter to the ground, she laid out the truth for him. Catherine had been watching from the ivy bank where she was busy weeding. "I'm not really supposed to talk to white people," the girl had said, picking up the bag and tucking it into her backpack. Catherine felt sad for both of them: John's shoulders visibly slumping, the girl shrugging as if in apology to John.

She felt sorry for herself too. Whenever Catherine heard the sounds of cookouts around Memorial Day time—from her back deck where she caught whiffs of the grilling meat and explosions of laughter—she felt a nagging sensation that she was missing something deep and meaningful by knowing only people like herself.

Catherine had always suspected that most people possessed a depth beyond hers, but particularly those people most unlike her. And this stirred a yearning in her that all the reading of literature and exploration of art museums and eager purchase of new music couldn't satisfy.

Still, she and John were at a loss at how to discuss this void, actual or perceived—much less fill it. They were tiring of the quest, whether they knew it directly or not, and after a year or two their house became just a nice place to live and not a progressive choice. And they forgot about their neighbors and went about their lives.

The summer of 2000 approached, a year in which they were making better salaries than they would have ever expected, salaries that could easily qualify them for houses in much more expensive neighborhoods. Yet they saved their money for future travels or lifestyle changes, and they focused now on their half-week summer getaway. They decided to stay at a bed and breakfast as they usually did, but instead of exploring the neighborhoods and art museums of their destination spot, as was their usual vacation habit, they planned to simply relax, to soak up the sun and sounds of the surf—and so they chose the relatively unglamorous town of Virginia Beach.

Catherine and John were pleasantly surprised when Stan and Simone, who were black, sat down to the first breakfast at Windsor cottage. Catherine realized she had never seen a black person at a bed and breakfast before.

The lack of diversity bothered Catherine. What bothered her even more was that, despite her usual sensitivity to matters of race, she had never before *noticed* this diversity problem of B and Bs. She wondered if her past obliviousness wasn't a sign of her own latent racism and she worried that her own vacations were a form of white flight.

Stan was describing the drive from Richmond, where he and Simone lived, when Charlie, their host, stepped in from the kitchen with the coffee pot, his loyal Doberman keeping herself pressed against his side as she seemed to do most of the time. "Stan, I thought you might be related to some people who were here last week, because they were also named Turner," he said, rubbing the dog's ears. "But they were Irish. You're not Irish are you?" The table laughed. Catherine had heard people laugh over the impossibility of white and black people being related so many times—on TV, in meetings with new staff members at work—she didn't know why it was so funny. Perhaps it was the laughter of relief, that someone had pointed out the obvious differences, however superficially.

Charlie's wife Gail entered the dining room with a plate of bacon and encouraged the group to dig in.

While they chatted about airports and city governments and the foods that were oddly popular in different cities—Jumbo bologna in Pittsburgh, pulled pork in Richmond—Catherine couldn't help but be nagged by an evaluation of her leisure time. But her preoccupation was causing her to miss parts of the conversation, so she forced herself to pay attention.

"Stonewall Jackson day?" John was saying, shoving a piece of bacon down with the animal quality he had when he was engrossed in conversation. When it came to John, Catherine had learned there was a fine balance between manners and enthusiasm.

"Well, the Richmond city council didn't give Jackson his own day. They just arranged it so it would fall on Martin Luther King day," Stan said.

"In case anyone was opposed to taking MLK off, they could take it off in Jackson's name," Simone said, a sparkle of irony in her eye.

"That's incredible!" she and John said, shaking their heads in unison, which upon noticing it, made Catherine feel absurd.

Why *did* she and John stay at places like this—such white places? And was there a way she could get the table to talk about it—-without sounding crass?

At work at the advertising firm where Catherine was an accountant, just the day before, she had mentioned that she was going to Virginia Beach for the weekend. Her co-worker had said, "Oh, the African American vacation haven!"

"Really?" Catherine asked. It was possible that the woman really knew, since she studied demographics as part of her marketing work.

The co-worker smirked. "We always go to Ocean City," she said. Catherine didn't pursue it; such innuendoes were common where she worked.

But now she saw, despite their efforts to live in a diverse neighborhood in Pittsburgh, that her usual vacation outings were largely devoid of black people, and she hoped that things may be about to change.

John lamented their lack of a car. "We didn't realize it was such a long beach! And this is the busy end."

"Well, we should have rented a car, but the walking will do us good," Catherine said, because she didn't want to sound like they were making a veiled plea for a ride.

"This is vacation, not a visit to the gym," Simone said. "You should come with us."

They settled into the leather seats of Stan's Land Rover and Catherine struggled for conversation starters other than environmentalism and gas guzzlers—but the subjects were as insistent in her mind as the vehicle was large. Stan and Simone weren't too concerned about the environment, that was clear.

"Stan used to spend time in the eighties section of the beach when he was just a wee boy," Simone said, touching Stan on the arm and smiling.

"My family came here every year until I was in my teens," he said. "It's a peaceful part of the beach."

"Tell us a Turner family story, Stan."

"I just did!" he laughed.

"You were stung by a jellyfish one year, you'll never forget, they had to use the beach towel as a stretcher to rush you to the hospital."

"No." Stan turned to roll his eyes at Catherine and John, but clearly he enjoyed Simone's imagination.

"Oh, come on Stan. Something must have happened! You and your siblings buried your dad in the sand one year and then forgot to dig him out—and he got sand lice! Or you built bonfires on the beach and roasted crabs you'd caught yourself. Or—oh, the memories—you used to build elaborate sand castles with the other children well into the evening. This is your youth and it's flooding over you today."

Imagining Stan as a little boy did seem humorous somehow—he had a wry expression that would never fit a child's face. They were all laughing now, the sound of it full and resonant in the large, leathery cab of the Land Rover.

"I had fun here. I remember that."

"Stan never gives me specifics," Simone said, nudging him. "We tried to get a room on the eighties, so Stan could better remember his youth, but we booked too late and ended up with the Windsor. It seems like a nice enough place. They're selling it, you know."

"No, I didn't. Did Gail or Charlie tell you?" John asked.

"No. It was on their Web site," Stan said.

"Gee," said John, and Catherine scowled at him. He saw her and mouthed "What?" which made her immediately sorry. But, what was with the one syllable commentary? They had to be coming off as horribly boring.

"I'm going to ask about it tomorrow morning," Simone said. "We'll probably find out more than we want to know. Maybe there's some deep horrible secret: like Charlie's actually gay, so Gail's getting a sex change operation that will force them to leave town."

John giggled uncontrollably. He was crazy about Simone, Catherine could tell. He leaned forward and held onto the back of Stan's seat, to get a better look at Simone, to say the things that would make her laugh. "Charlie worked for some high powered division of IBM for 50 years, but now that he's retired, he's worried that he missed the information age. He was asking me all these questions about dot-coms. I didn't want to break it to him that the New Economy is over," John said.

"Sounds like a real visionary," Stan said, in his dry fashion that Catherine found attractive. Stan drove his vehicle with a reclined confidence so unlike John, who she sometimes teased, calling him a hood ornament. John liked to be prepared, his seat back erect and his hands firmly on the wheel at ten and two o'clock.

"It takes a village, people," Simone called out to the slow-moving traffic of tourists.

Stan zipped through the snarl and Catherine was reminded of her father's comment the last time she had visited her parents in Florida. "The blacks — the black men — they're very aggressive drivers." Catherine wondered now, why her father often had some insight about black people, when he never associated with them and rarely saw them.

"Take it easy on the company car," Simone warned him, and Catherine felt ashamed that she had assumed he was anti-environment. He couldn't help what car corporate America wanted to lay on him.

They unloaded the Land Rover of the beach chairs and cooler and their bags. Catherine noticed the ultra-pleased smile that was directed to them from families unpacking their cars nearby. She felt her anger flare at the approving, almost relieved expressions reserved especially for the rare spectacle of interracial couples out and about together. What right did these white families have to tender their appreciative glances? Perhaps they were just happy to leave racial harmony to the rest of the world.

The sand on Virginia Beach was soft and smooth, and even though it was the Fourth of July weekend, there wasn't too much of a crowd.

Now Catherine looked across the beach and saw no more blacks than the twelve percent national average, despite her co-worker's description of Virginia Beach.

And here they were, two couples out for relaxation on the beach, black and white, professional, healthy, well adjusted. Maybe the subtext didn't have to be this loaded, but it was, wasn't it? At least it was for Catherine, who hadn't done much mingling with blacks, and who couldn't seem to stop smarting at the realization.

Catherine remembered a visit from an old friend who had moved to Portland and been living there for a few years. "I miss Pittsburgh!" she had exclaimed, as they sat on the front porch relaxing with a bottle of red wine. "You see black people here! You never see them in Portland!"

"Yeah. But we don't know any. We just see them."

"Still, that's something. I mean you never see them in Portland!"

At the time, the wine made it hard for Catherine to understand why her friend's comment bothered her. But in hindsight she saw that her friend's attitude sounded like reassurance at the sight of endangered animals, like appreciating their value, but from a distance informed by caution, or fear.

Simone walked a few strides ahead of Catherine, dragging her raft behind her, her calves sparkling with droplets of water.

Catherine's heart swelled with well-being and satisfaction; she hadn't felt this happy in months. She and Simone threw their rafts next to the men and began a long walk up the beach together, talking the usual stuff: weight issues and home improvement projects and pets and parents. Catherine told her story about how for years she had believed "Mares Eat Oats" was a song in gibberish, and Simone laughed, as people always did. It was the sweet, self-deprecating kind of the story that made Catherine likeable.

They stopped to examine a barnacled piece of driftwood tangled with seaweed. "There's little crabs in there," a white girl stopped to tell them in her breathless voice, picking her bathing suit from her crack.

"There's a whole world of life in this log," Simone said, pulling her finger away from a barnacle as it slowly closed.

"I know," the little girl said, and ran back into the surf.

Catherine laughed. "Little Miss Crabs better watch her step."

They walked on, resuming their conversation. Simone talked about her cousin who had just come back from a yearlong stay in Italy, about how the culture shock was stunning for her, because people were in such a hurry here in the States. Catherine couldn't help wondering where Simone's poor Mississippi Delta relatives were. Didn't she have any cousins with six or seven children, living on welfare? Wasn't it just a fact of black American life?

Catherine tried to find those characters in Simone's life by talking about her own sister, Barbie, who lived in a trailer park with four kids, whose husband had left her after losing his job. "She isn't interested in birth control, I guess," Catherine said, but Simone didn't seem to have a comparable story. She acted as surprised as any white person by Barbie's ramshackle life.

By noon the sun was directly over their heads and beating an extra pulse into Catherine's blood. Catherine had a dark corner and a beer in mind. She and John insisted on treating for lunch somewhere, but Stan and Simone declined, as if to suggest offense at John and Catherine's implication that repayment might be expected. "We're just hanging out," said Stan. He opened up the cooler, offered each of them a sandwich, then returned to his book.

Stan was reading a contemporary black, male novelist. John asked about the book and Stan explained that it wasn't exactly a political commentary on anything — just black people in a black culture. Something about a guy thinking about his ex-girlfriends.

Nevertheless, Catherine was embarrassed by her book, a really white comic romp called *Happy All the Time.* She had bought it at the airport, because she wanted something mindless. Now she hoped no one would ask her about it. *Lives Without Black People,* the book should have been called.

The words on the page marched by as she tried to think where she most often saw black people having a good time. She could think of the city pool, where she had recently gone when her mother was visiting Pittsburgh, and been very aware of her mother's prim reaction. And of course she had also seen blacks at leisure in the backyards throughout her neighborhood, where on Saturdays the rich smoke from cooking meat was the norm.

But she and John had vacationed many places, even in just the time since their wedding five years ago: Toronto for shopping in the fall, Florida for the beach in the winter, hiking in Boulder, the road trip on Route 66, the quick trip to Madrid, on and on and very few black people that she could remember. Were they able to vacation much? She had never thought of it, but acknowledged now that without a nice income, leisure must be limited – at least as Catherine knew it. She decided to go back to work on Monday and find out more about African American leisure time from the people in marketing.

She looked at her companions, Stan with his book, Simone with her closed eyelids shining in the sun, adjusting her earphones, and Catherine realized that they probably weren't thinking about black or white issues.

Why, for Catherine, had every single prop, every comment, every grain of sand become so charged with subtext just because she and John were spending the day together with a black couple?

She tried to explain it to John later, after their showers and before dinner.

"Things aren't charged like you think!" he said. "They're charged because we like them so much! They're nice. Remember how we fell in love with Roy and Cristina?"

It was true, it felt like their old friends Roy and Cristina. Each little thing seemed to hold importance: knuckle cracking, the playful slant to a raised eyebrow, the way they knocked on the door, everything they did was lovable and fun.

"But, it's not just that," she said. "There's a subtext to our lives that we don't think about. The book I'm reading, it acts like there is no racism, like there are no black people period."

"It's not a topic of that particular book. You're getting too worked up over this."

"But why is race a topic? It shouldn't be a topic. There are white people and black people. It's not a topic, it's reality."

"Catherine, there are men and women, and that's reality. And it's still a topic in some things you read." His hand slipped between her thighs. "I've got a topic if you want to discuss it," he said with a growl that made her giggle.

Later she lay in the tub, blowing bubbles off her palm as she'd seen people do in television commercials, and thought about Simone and Stan. How they were so normal, so relaxed. How, before getting to know them, she wouldn't have guessed bed and breakfasts on the beach were how they spent their leisure time. If someone had asked her at breakfast, she might have said that she pictured them in heated debates about politics, debates with complicated, loaded thoughts dripping with footnotes and ironic asides, like the cultural theory textbooks she had studied in college. She realized that she also had assumed earlier that Stan and Simone had some connection to the travails of the inner city—that Simone would have to answer the phone during one of her political discussions to take in the news of a drive-by near her cousin's house in the projects, that maybe she would go to the hospital and help in whatever way she could, only to return to the continued discussions with Stan and their political elite friends, discussions that took place over the labeling of important newsletters or the planning of African American solidarity events.

And it was ridiculous to imagine that anyone would have such a representative life. Yet this was a burden she had fully expected Stan and Simone to take on, while she went about her easy, non-political life.

They dined separately that evening, which was good, since John and Catherine were terrified of outwearing their welcome. Later Catherine and John sat in the study of the Windsor, digesting their dinners and cuddling by the dim light of the faux gas lamps.

"Gail and Charlie are in the Christian Bed and Breakfast guide," John said, pointing out the listing in the large paperback he had pulled from the shelves.

"Stan and Simone aren't married. I'm surprised Gail and Charlie let them stay here, being Christian pillars of society and all," John continued, putting the book on the coffee table beside him. "Did you hear Charlie tell Simone this morning that the pet Doberman favored her because they're the same color?"

"God! He compared her color to the dog's?"

"Right."

"Oh," Catherine put her head in her hands. She was embarrassed for Gail and Charlie, and yet, they were no more related to her than they were to Simone.

"They're just like all our friends, only better, funnier," John said.

"It's gross we don't have any black friends at home," Catherine whispered, her breath sounding harsh in the cozy study.

"Why is that, anyway?"

"Our lives are like bed and breakfasts," Catherine said. "Black people don't come into them very often."

"And when they do come in, they're not really from black culture," John said, his voice wavering like a candle as he tried to keep it to a whisper. "They're just like all the white professionals we know."

"Why should we dictate their lifestyle? Isn't *that* racist?"

"It's racist that we're not doing anything to get to know *real* black culture, when it's right here in America. We lead soap opera lives where everybody makes decent money and everybody is healthy and white. Makes me want to walk up the street to the Pig's Foot diner every Sunday for a real lunch with black people."

"We don't make friends just to learn about 'other cultures' from them," Catherine reminded him. Then, afraid she had been too harsh, she added, "I wonder how they can continue to live in Richmond?"

"To put up with all that racist crap. To hear them talk, they're pretty tolerant of Confederate pride."

"God, can you believe Richmond declared Martin Luther King day Stonewall Jackson day also? What a slap in the face."

"Really," John said, and Catherine vowed that she would read about Stonewall Jackson when she returned home. She had no doubt that John knew plenty about Jackson, but she was embarrassed to ask him for the whole story. She didn't want him to start thinking that she was the reason they led such white lives.

"I like how we didn't talk politics all day," Catherine commented, thinking really how strange it was to have politics such a constant and intense subtext.

"They follow it. They knew about the Johnny Gammage case in Pittsburgh. But they seem a far cry from activists."

Catherine didn't like his disapproving tone. She could see why they would just want to live their lives, rather than buck such an old, ridiculous social structure, one that was bound to crumble eventually anyway. "We don't have time to be activists. Should we really demand that of our black friends?" she said. Women were discriminated against on a daily basis, after all, but Catherine didn't do much to fight that. She even let sexist comments slide from time to time, not feeling up to the minor confrontation sure to ensue.

"It *is* strange that we haven't seen African Americans at any of the bed and breakfasts we've gone to before," John thought aloud.

"It's really brought to my attention how our vacations are so very white," said Catherine, listening to the sound of the creaking steps above them. Someone was coming downstairs. "That we don't have a diverse set of friends."

"But think about who your sister is," John said. "Would you be her friend if she wasn't your sister?"

"Probably not, and yet she's my best friend."

Despite their differences, Catherine thought Barbie was the funniest person she knew; they had hour-long conversations every week.

"So we know we're *capable* of being friends with people different than us. But it's our habit to fall in love with those who are just like us."

"Narcissists."

"We figured it out."

"We're so smart."

"I know. I love us."

They giggled quietly. Then Gail appeared in the doorway.

"Do you have everything you need in your room?" she asked, wiping her hands on her shorts and looking around.

"Yes, the stay has been wonderful!" Catherine noticed that her voice was near a whisper, but somehow it felt right for the intimacy of the dim study, the potential that Charlie was sleeping, and that Stan and Simone would be back soon from dinner.

"We heard that you're selling the Windsor," John said, just like that, direct as possible. Catherine pinched him gently, under the cover of their entwined limbs.

"That Internet!" Gail exclaimed, shaking her head. "You think you're targeting to your market, but then your clients find out what you're up to."

"Well, it doesn't make our stay any less pleasant!" Catherine said. "I imagine running a B and B is hard work. I don't know if I could always be the host to so many different kinds of people."

Catherine could feel herself slipping into a mode of semi-espionage, where she asked leading questions of white people whom she suspected of racism. After Charlie's weird comment about the dog, she figured she had some evidence. She wanted Gail to say the thing that uncovered the who behind the racism, that put a face to the nameless illness that was America. But there was a problem with the game—namely that it helped perpetuate the idiotic sentiments. She knew this because she herself never stopped the interrogated on the first questionable comment. She waited for something juicier, some admission about Klan membership or a comparison between blacks and monkeys.

"It really is hard work," Gail said. "And yet, we've been bitten by the B and B bug. We're going to open another one on Deep Creek Lake in Maryland."

"We've been there!" Catherine said, changing her mind, resolving to veer away from her destructive course. "That's a beautiful place."

"Of course you've been there. And mark my words, you'll go there more than Virginia Beach as you get older. It's a different world there. More relaxed. Virginia Beach is perfect for the younger set. As you are older though, you feel overwhelmed by so much activity. You look for a slower pace."

"There do seem to be a lot of teenagers on the strip," John said sympathetically, and Catherine wondered if he was playing the game. She had seen him lead conversations to that dreaded destination in the past.

"There are a lot of different kinds of people here now," Gail nodded.

Catherine felt the effort John exerted not to glance over at her.

"I get along fine with most people," Gail continued. "But sometimes, there is an element, there is some aggressive behavior. You just turn on the local news and you can see it. My guests are saying Virginia Beach is not the place they used to come to. It's changed. A lot of rap music in the cars going by, you know, that kind of stuff."

"Do you get many black people as guests?" Catherine said, her appetite peaked, her willpower gone, and ready for Gail to dish out the main course.

"Oh, no. They prefer the high rise hotels near the beach, where they can cram ten kids in there with them and play that awful music into the wee hours."

"Not your typical clientele," Catherine said.

"Certainly not."

But John was calling it quits. "Everybody parties down from time to time, don't they Gail?"

"Well, we don't really have to worry about that, thank God, this being a B and B, but sometimes the music from the cars on the streets, it trickles in. Guests notice. They say it's not the same. And they're right." She paused, pulling yellow leaves thoughtfully off the houseplant on the windowsill. "Don't get me wrong. I'm not talking about people like Stan and Simone."

Catherine hated herself and John for their sympathetic nods, their refusal to make the moral statement, after they had nudged the conversation there. It was wrong. It was wrong to uncover the problem with the engine, only to let the hood slam back down. But political conversations in genteel surroundings seemed wrong too, and she found herself once again fenced in by conventions. She was sick of being so damned appropriate.

So even leisure spots had white flight, Catherine thought, sitting alone on the Windsor front porch, watching the sun rise over the trees that blocked her view of the beach.

Whites just didn't want to vacation around black people, she decided, running the loose end of her robe's belt through her fingers. During her mother's recent visit to Pittsburgh, when Catherine had taken her to the city pool, it had become apparent that her mother had probably never been around so many black people at one time. Catherine had decided it was a good experience for her mother.

"I haven't been to a city pool in thirty years probably," her mother had said, looking around her with an uncertain smile. She skimmed the top of the water with her fingernails. A black boy swimming underwater rammed into her mother's leg and popped up, sputtering water and wiping at his fogged goggles.

"Watch where you're going," her mother said, with a trace of condescension.

She scanned the expanse of dark bobbing heads in the crystal blue water and looked at Catherine. "It's nice. It's nice for people to be able to have some fun and stay cool."

She approved, Catherine thought, with a shudder of distaste for her mother. This was as it should be, the woman was probably thinking — the play behind chain link, the organization of the mob. Wild places, like beaches and mountains and forests, places her mother preferred for relaxation, those were reserved for white people. But this was nice for the blacks.

Catherine and her mother had exited the pool and sunned on their towels. Catherine flipped onto her stomach and examined the peaceful, lined face of her mother's. Mascara was bleeding around her mother's closed eyes. She had flat shiny spots on her skin where two moles had been removed.

"Did I just hear the word 'snatch'?" her mother asked, her eyes still closed. The music that piped out above them had a good beat, but it was not a band Catherine knew.

Catherine laughed. "I don't know. Probably."

Why did she have any right to judge her mother? she had wondered at that moment. Catherine might be more comfortable than the woman to swim in a pool with black people, but was she any more moral a person? She would probably never make a friend with any black person here. The women her age were all here with small children. They had long, ornately painted fingernails that Catherine found tacky, if not comical, especially the time she saw a woman struggle not to pop her child's inflated arm bands as she pulled them on the boy. She sometimes found these women rude, the way they barely moved to let her pass on the pool steps, the way the black gate attendants always had to finish their long conversation about a coming wedding or their church or their baby's sleep habits before they could look up at her pool tag to let her in. And all they had to do was look at the tag. But instead they had to let her feel rude, like an eavesdropper on their conversation.

The blacks had children and she didn't. They had church and she didn't. They had complicated hairstyles and she didn't. But of course, the biggest difference was that they didn't have money and she did.

Most of the white people she knew paid exorbitant fees to go to private pools at country clubs. Catherine went to the public pool, partly because it was less expensive, and partly because, even if she didn't interact with the black people, she liked to be reminded that they were there.

So she was no different from her Portland friend who was relieved at the sight of Pittsburgh's black people. With her mother here, Catherine felt the oddest sense that something would happen, that somehow the two worlds would collide and that a conflict would ensue. Wasn't it racist to be so uncomfortable bringing your white mother around black people? Wasn't she the one with the problem? When, after all, she was the one who couldn't relax.

She sighed thinking of it. She noted that she had intricately woven the terry cloth around the fingers of her left hand. The ends of her fingers were beginning to throb.

Simone and Catherine threw themselves down on the beach towels next to their men. Catherine had the strongest urge to grab Simone's hand. They had just spent an exhilarating hour bodysurfing and Catherine's skin absolutely buzzed. She loved the crazed look that Simone got before they dove toward shore and so she decided to tell her so. "You get the craziest look on your face before diving in. It's so funny!" she said.

Simone's smile was a bit distracted, or maybe chilly. Catherine worried that she had hurt Simone's feelings, that she was losing the camaraderie as fast as she had gained it on the waves.

"You should have heard the conversation we were having with Gail last night," Catherine blurted out. "I think we figured out why they're selling the Windsor."

"Yeah, they seem to think there's an 'element' moving into Virginia Beach," John said, tossing his copy of *Harper's* aside, more excited to talk about this than Catherine would have expected.

"What does that mean?" Stan asked with mild interest.

"Well, they did have a thing or two to say about rap music," said Catherine, feeling suddenly sheepish. She wondered if she should admit that she and John had given the conversation with Gail a little push in the racist direction.

"They did act really surprised to find we were black," Simone said to Stan, as if that provided additional evidence.

"You're black?" John asked. They all laughed, although Catherine hated that kind of joke. It brought forth, again, the kind of relieved laughter that came when someone vocalized what was on everyone's mind: the differences, the possibly irreconcilable differences.

"I like Gail, though," Simone said. "She's funny."

Catherine felt an irrational and jealous urge to set Simone straight about Gail. "No, really. She's not exactly into diversity. And how can she let Charlie go around comparing you to their dog?"

"Oh, please, that was no insult. That dog is a beautiful color! They love that dog like a member of their family!"

"That's not why they're selling the Windsor, though," said Stan. "They're not getting enough business, white or black. There are two rooms open this weekend. Those vacancies have got to hurt."

It was true. Stan was reasonable. Catherine found herself gazing at him and Simone interchangeably. Then, worried they could feel her watching them, she opened her book.

That night, she heard them come in from their dinner together —she and John had already been back from dinner for an hour—and she got out of bed. She crept down the stairs and heard Stan and Charlie talking in the study. She tied her robe tighter around her and knocked lightly at the open door.

"Hey!" Stan said, patting the seat of the couch near him. "We just came from the Magnolia Pub. It was really nice."

"We ate at the Raven tonight," she said. She wasn't sure that she wanted to join them—how could you discuss anything important with Charlie around? And now, seeing Charlie and Stan in this intimate setting, she felt ashamed that she and

John had all but called Charlie and Gail racists earlier—so she leaned against the doorway.

"It's nice how well you four have gotten along," said Charlie. "We don't see that often with our guests. But when we do, well, it's really the reason you become the proprietor of a B and B, to bring people together."

Catherine nodded, feeling somehow shamed by Charlie's words.

"The sun tired me out today," Stan said, stretching. "Simone wanted to go to the disco, but I told her to forget it. I'm too spent."

"I haven't gone to the disco once since we've been here," Catherine said.

"It's within walking distance. Why don't you see if she still wants to go?"

"Hmm, well, I came down here for a book," Catherine lied, reaching for the guide to bed and breakfasts, "but maybe I'll check on her enthusiasm level."

She bumped into John as he came out of the hall shower. She explained that she might go to the disco, which sounded foreign coming from her lips. He half-smiled and said he hoped she didn't mind going without him.

She tapped on Simone's door and it opened, Simone's gorgeous eyes luminous in the dim light. "Sit down!" Simone said, backing away from the door and welcoming her in. Catherine took the rocking chair, ignoring the towel slung over the bentwood, and Simone quickly straightened the bedspread and sat on it.

"Stan is having some deep conversation with Charlie," Catherine said, giggling.

"Maybe he's negotiating a price for the B and B," Simone laughed.

"I thought maybe we could talk, and maybe go to the disco," Catherine said.

"Yeah?" Simone said, bouncing a little on the bed and looking curious.

Catherine considered easing into the conversation, but something told her to jump in instead, for the fear that she would never get to the point. "I'm so frustrated, because, and I know this sounds stupid, but I have never had the chance to really know some black people, to really be friends."

"Mmm," Simone said, and Catherine tried not to read anything into it.

"And here we have the chance, and I don't want to blow it by being too weird."

The next thing she knew, Catherine was telling her story about the time when she had been waitressing, back when she actually had the occasion to sit around and drink and chat with black people, and how she had screwed it up. She relayed an example of an after-work chat she'd had with a black cook. They were talking about jitnies and she mentioned how she had taken a jitney once, how she had been pretty nervous about it. The co-worker nodded with an air of understanding, which she took as his automatic assumption that she would be afraid of a black driver. "Oh no, the driver wasn't black," she said, meaning to say that she would have been nervous no matter what, that race wasn't an issue here. But he had taken it to mean that she would have been *especially* scared if the jitney driver was black. He excused himself, saying he needed to get home, leaving a nearly full beer sweating on the table. She had tried to apologize the next day, but he ignored her, going past her to the basement with a sloshing bucket of pickles.

Halfway through her story, Catherine began to worry that Simone had heard this kind of white person confession before.

"Yeah, it's not easy," Simone said, sighing.

"You seem weary of these kinds of stories," Catherine said.

"I am. I'm weary. I'm weary of white guilt and I'm weary of black defensiveness. Let's go to the disco," she said. She opened the wardrobe and pulled out two beautiful beach wraps. "We'll make blouses of these," she said.

Catherine loosened her robe and wrapped a pink and black flowered silk around her top, handkerchief style. "I live in a mixed neighborhood," she said, trying to avoid a defensive tone. "I try, but I never get to know any black people. What is with that?"

"That looks good," Simone said. "Put on some shorts or jeans and you'll be ready."

The residential streets around the Windsor were dusted with sand at the edges, giving every corner an ornamental fringe. It filled Catherine's sandals and made the bottoms of her feet feel raw. They crossed two busy streets and were on the boardwalk, where even at 11:30 at night many people were still out walking, rollerblading or leaning on the railing smoking cigarettes.

The ferris wheel at the tiny amusement park was quiet and unlit, though, and the overflowing garbage cans hinted at a much larger mass of people processed here in the daylight hours.

"I dated a white guy for awhile," Simone said. "His family had trouble with it. So did mine. I don't think we're far enough from segregation to be comfortable being together."

"It's true that our parents remember segregation. I've asked my mother about it. She just says 'that's the way it was. I worked at Burger King and would serve the black people out the back door. I was always polite to them. It's where they came to get their food, like the delivery people brought the Coke canisters to the back door. I never thought about it. I was just trying to make a living.' And you know, you just don't pursue it, because you don't want to hate your own parents for being so blind to injustice."

"You don't want to hate your parents for being so passive about it either," Simone said.

"There are still so many injustices," Catherine said. "Mainly economic, I guess. I don't have a lot in common with my neighbors and I think it's because I make a lot more money than they do. I don't want to seem fake, acting like there aren't any differences between us. So then it's like I just can't get past those differences, not far enough to make a real connection."

The tide was visible on the horizon, a pale blue twist of foam like a scarf caught forever in the wind. Bikers, couples strolling, older people sitting on benches, it seemed everyone had a mildly interested glance reserved for Simone and Catherine.

They found a spot at the disco bar and got comfortable. Catherine felt cognizant of her white shoulders next to Simone's. She thought the contrast probably looked pretty good together, the two young women in their beach wraps. They were getting glances from men walking by.

"It's been really fun hanging out with you two," Simone said, leaning in and yelling over the music. "We'll have to exchange email addresses."

Catherine agreed. "Absolutely," she said, straightening the shell bracelet on Simone's wrist. The shells looked like the puffy, wrinkled mouths of old women, lined up and urging her to talk to Simone. She felt their boardwalk conversation needed closure. "Anyway," she yelled, hoping she wasn't spitting on Simone's shoulders. "I sometimes get really depressed by the fact that I don't have any black friends."

"Well, it saves you from making the 'I have lots of

black friends' comment," Simone said, leaning back and smiling.

"Yeah, I guess," Catherine said, nodding and taking a sip from her drink. Simone's comment sounded as though Catherine could use all available help to avoid making racist comments.

"Don't feel bad," Simone said, twirling her tiny drink umbrella. She leaned in and Catherine examined the loose curls of hair at her nape. "Stan and I don't really have any white friends."

"But. I mean, you stay at bed and breakfasts! You seem so…"

"White? So much like you?" Simone's yell seemed more hoarse now. She seemed a little turned off. "We do lots of things that black people don't often do, like go hiking in the mountains. You should see the scared look on white people's faces when they run into us on a deserted mountain path."

"Oh God," Catherine said, embarrassed again for the dolts in her race.

"But then, we made friends with this family once, on a mountain stay at a cabin in the Smoky Mountains. They were fun, but by the end of the trip we had come to the conclusion that they didn't think we were black enough."

"How rude. How did you know?" Catherine said, feeling dreadfully confident that she and John had come off the same way.

"Oh, one night it was sort of late and they played some Black Sheep and went on and on about how moving the lyrics were. Stan yawned and it seemed to really piss them off. I mean, yeah, we like rap and we're glad that they did too, but we're not that wild about Black Sheep. Big deal, right? And why didn't they play Patsy Cline for us? We like her too."

"Ugh." It seemed suddenly horrible that they were yelling these stories to each other. Catherine no longer wanted to chat and yet Simone continued.

"Some white people, they want to take the diversity thing a little too far," Simone said, her breath warm on Catherine's ear. "They want representatives of the hood; they don't want middle class blacks to be their black friends."

Catherine shook her head, perhaps a little too vehemently, looking into the slushy pinkness of her drink, like wet, pink sand. There was a beach on an island somewhere in the Caribbean where the sand was pink, she had heard. The billions of tiny shrimp local to the area gave the sand that pink color. She wished they had gone there instead and not met these nice people who she'd probably disgusted with her stupid behavior.

"But I think white people just feel bad that they've never gotten to know blacks," Catherine tried to explain, still looking down, not sure if Simone could hear her. "They meet a couple like you and they think, 'That was too easy. I haven't fulfilled my duty yet. I need to get to know a wider range of blacks to really understand the black experience.'"

"Look, I may not have much in common with the blacks in the poorest neighborhoods in Pittsburgh. But we've all got our discrimination story. Every black person in this country has a story."

"What's yours?" Catherine asked, maybe too eagerly.

"I don't want to talk about it, really."

A guy passed them and lingered. Catherine shook her head at him and he moved on with a shrug. She felt deeply snubbed that Simone wouldn't tell her story.

"Look, maybe you and I are dabbling, you know?" Simone said, her voice straining. "Maybe the point is that we have to do some long term work on this. We need to go back to our cities and find friends from the other race. Maybe it's easy for us to be so accepting of each other because we know it's short term."

"Do you feel like you needed to make concessions in order to like me?" Catherine asked.

"No, Catherine, God!" Simone looked heavenward.

"Well, what do you mean? I don't feel that way about you, but, if you've been 'accepting' me, I want to know in spite of what."

"OK, to be fair. I think it's sort of strange, I mean, I don't know if I could handle being so closely listened to all the time. I feel like an ambassador, like whatever I say or do will be reported in tomorrow's paper as 'the voice of American blacks.' It's a little disconcerting. It's easy to relax despite it while I'm on vacation, but if I was at home, if I knew in my everyday life that I was being watched like this, that my ratings were constantly going up or down—"

"I got it," Catherine said, laughing her way around the hurt. "To defend myself: I think it was more a 'crush' on you and Stan and less an obsession with your opinions as blacks."

"Never mind. It was just a feeling I got. But I've felt it before from whites, and it's just too much pressure. Or maybe that's not it. Maybe it's how you and John tried to so hard to differentiate yourselves from Gail and Charlie, who are just average white people, not rampant racists. Look, I don't want to talk about this. We're dancing, already," Simone said, taking Catherine's arm and pulling her through the tightness of the crowd.

They danced alternately with each other and with men on the floor. Catherine was relieved not to have to look anyone in the eye, to scan the room and move her body, and not care how she looked or where she looked. She was as inhuman as the lights in the room, the blobs of red and blue forming and dissolving in lazy circles.

It was her life. It was what it was. She would dance here tonight with Simone and they would walk home quietly with just a comment or two about what people were wearing at the disco or what that one crazy guy had said. They were buzzed and not concerned with conversation or maybe they were exhausted from conversation. They would exchange email addresses later that night but neither would write to the other. John would start having lunch at the Pig's Foot diner in an effort to make friends with the real blacks of Pittsburgh and Catherine would get irritated with the dudes (John always called black men "dudes") who occasionally stopped by at nine at night with hands stuffed into pockets of windbreakers and asking for John or just a couple of bucks or at least a drink of water. She eventually tired of dropping what she was doing, inviting them in for tea and pitying them and concealing her yawns (which were from genuine exhaustion) through a drunken sob story again. She and John would have a baby and she would start turning John's few diner friends away without water or tea or anything at all because the baby was trying to sleep or the baby was teething or the baby had an ear infection. They were busier all the time and John's promotion and Catherine's promotion had them working around the clock and their nanny was Dominican and that was another culture to think about but never fully know, although they absolutely *loved* Paola and would do anything for her. And they would move into a bigger house although they were still very committed to the city and so they stayed within the city limits and paid their exorbitant city taxes and yet agonized over sending their daughter to private school or possibly the magnet Montessori school which was public and fifty percent black.

Then one evening they were at a PTA meeting, having made the decision to go with public school, and they met a black couple, rather wealthy liberal Democrat professionals and patrons of the symphony and ballet.

And Catherine thought perhaps this was finally her chance, seven years later, finally her chance and she played it cool. She had some easy, banal conversation with the black woman that night and felt there was promise that perhaps at the next PTA meeting they would exchange phone numbers. That night in bed, her daughter finally asleep, John already snoring next to her, she imagined that she was on the verge of making her first true black friends in Pittsburgh, and that they might remain friends with her and John all their lives. And Catherine thought that she would be able to thank Simone for that—Simone and her honesty— and Catherine was simultaneously humbled and proud. She was humbled by what seemed to be an overarching plan: such a deep friendship was about to develop because of the wisdom Simone had imparted to Catherine. And she was proud that she had learned something, that she hadn't been crushed by Simone's words but had resolved to keep them with her until she could use them for something good. She was further awed that every interaction in a life has a potential purpose. And she thought about digging up Simone's email address, which she still had, tucked away in her jewelry box, and writing Simone a note about having reached the brink of that long-term effort to make friends with the other race. Then she realized how insane it would sound, that seven years had passed and *finally* she was only on the verge of *possibly* making black friends, and she was filled with a burning shame.

Cool Moms

JENNIFER BANNAN

At the pool I watch the teenagers. They're sexy and tan and foulmouthed. I'm still young, only in my early twenties. The years from fifteen to twenty-two are long, though, and I remember myself as though I were a different person then. I remember how mature I thought I was, how confident. These are East Tennessee teenagers, not the city kids I grew up with in Miami. Even so, these kids look more sophisticated than I was at their age. They move better, they have throaty laughter. They intimidate.

I'm visiting my grandparents in Sevierville, where they retired when I was a child. I hope to gain some insight from them, before they're gone, before I have my baby, who is due in five months. I spent summers of my youth here, but never came to this pool back then, preferring to read in the wooded backyard or to write letters to my boyfriend at home.

Somehow, though, during this visit, I've found myself at the pool every day. I find it difficult to tear myself away from watching the teens.

One girl here, in particular, captures my interest. She has round elbows and a toothy white smile. Boys at school probably make fun of her for being a bit heavy, but I can tell she has no trouble getting kissed when she wants it. She has the kind of intelligent eyes that make parents nervous. She catches my eye and flashes that smile. She knows I like to watch her. She reminds me of myself at her age.

Two weeks after my fifteenth birthday, my mother found a condom in the toilet when she came home from work. I couldn't deny it, as she opened up a Kleenex and showed me the Trojan wrapper. You could ruin your life, she had said. What about college? What about your future? She begged me to tell her what I would do if I were to get pregnant. I cried and told her I wouldn't know what to do. But that was a lie. Four weeks before, I had gone to the clinic near the mall for a pregnancy test, and when the gum-popping clinician told me I was positive, I said I wanted an abortion. I scheduled it so that I wouldn't even have to skip school. During the week between the test and the final procedure, I had morning sickness, and threw up in the backyard every morning while my parents got ready for work. The dog sniffed the bile at my feet and licked it up. He looked at me with guilty eyes. "Don't hate me for bringing you into this," I'd tell him.

My boyfriend José, who was seventeen, had suggested keeping the baby. He cried more often than I did; he said, please, we'll get married. I knew I would never marry this boy, who would go on to join the Navy, who would lead a simple life. I was of a better mold. I would not ruin my future. He knew all of these things, but he tried. If he could only make me feel the baby as much as he felt, deep down, the coming end of our relationship.

But he couldn't. After the abortion, we went to McDonald's and ate Chicken McNuggets. The next day in gym class, I had trouble running laps. My legs were cramped and heavy.

All of the things we knew would happen happened. After he joined the Navy, we drifted apart. I went to college and met Mo, the father of the baby I'm carrying now. I didn't plan on this baby either, but I'll be keeping it.

As much as I want to focus on the excitement of this pregnancy, I'm tripped up by the way life's decisions seem ugly and calculated. Mo is successful and José wasn't. Mo has the college education and corporate management position with a pharmaceutical firm, a job José would never have dreamed about. It seems cruel to my high school love—or at least classist—that I should be having a baby now for Mo, a man who already has plenty in his life. It seems cruel that I should go through with it now, when the elapsed seven years leave me feeling no more prepared.

Mo may be a success, but I'm another story. A year behind him in college, I graduated at the height of the recession, when the jobs were not exactly plentiful. I've been waiting tables in Pittsburgh, where we live. I've been loving the break from college, the mindless job, but my mother's questions about my resume, about interviews, about whether or not I should wear a navy or black suit, leave me guilty. I haven't searched particularly well. And now this. My mother will be disappointed. She had aspirations for me.

Not that I'm not getting cold feet. I want the baby. I love Mo. We can do it. Anyway, I'm already four months along. There's not much turning back at this point. I just feel so dreamy. So strange, like this isn't happening.

The plump, teenage girl with wild hair puts her elbow on the boy's shoulder and leans casually. He makes a remark and laughs. His eyes are waiting, frightened, simple like my dog's. Her eyes pull into a slant and she moves her mouth around a sexy comeback. The others laugh. He can't compete with her. She's too much for him. He's just a passing thing for her.

I get up from my towel and leave the public pool. It's much later than I told my grandmother I would return.

My grandmother didn't ask a single question about my coming here. To her it seemed to make all the sense in the world. Mo thought it was strange, wondering why I wouldn't want to learn about parenting from my own parents. But my parents have never seemed very nurturing, and they're so committed to their careers, they wouldn't have time to visit with me.

In the house, my grandfather sits in his rocker eating the BLT my grandmother has made for him. He asks me about the pool. How was the pool?

I ask him how the TV has been. He doesn't resent my question. He knows what he's all about. He is resigned. He's almost never drunk, but last night he was, and he and I talked about the war. It's amazing to me that his best stories are from the war, when he was at the age I'm at now. He has nothing better to tell after that. The war stories aren't even very good. He was never in combat, because of his bad knees. He drove supplies from place to place in his jeep, on back roads, never in any more danger than the civilians and their children. Mostly his stories are about jeep failures, about getting stuck in the mud. Last night I asked him, what about since then? What can you tell me about your life since the war?

I didn't know about his sadness until this visit. He tells me that he thinks his life has been a failure. Pop-pop says, "There hasn't been much I can be proud of."

He tells me he's proud of his children. They're his only success.

We watch the TV for awhile and then my grandmother comes in from the shed. She shows us what she's been busy making: a wooden jewelry box with flowers and hearts carved into the lid. "She sure is something," Pop-pop says.

I lie in bed in my grandparents' guest room and think of José, whose baby I didn't have. When he graduated from high school, he had nothing he wanted to do, and nothing he was very good at doing. The last time I heard from him he was in his last year at the Navy. He called me at my dorm room in college. I was quite the elitist—self-assured, even smug in tone. Would he go back home, after he was out? Back to Miami, where we had grown up together, and live with his parents? He wasn't sure. But how had it been in the Navy? Did he have a girlfriend? No, but he had a motorcycle. He took long drives and was seeing a lot of the West Coast. He left me saying he missed me and hoped we would see each other again. Maybe I would write to him.

It surprises me how much time I've spent thinking about the Navy boy, but I now realize my grandparent's house has a lot to do with it. The last summer before he left for the Navy, I shocked him by spending three long weeks at my grandparent's house, as I had done every childhood summer before him. "You act as if our time together's not precious," he said, stunned that I would go away right after the abortion, and right before he would leave for his new life in the military.

I lie in bed and hope his life has found some success somewhere. There will be other babies for him. This is a gift so many women give to the men they love. A gift that can often mean success. I know my grandparents' four fine children are fine and good primarily because my grandmother made them so. Men didn't meddle with children in my grandfather's time, and yet, this is his life success, his children with whom he had very little to do.

My grandmother wakes me in the morning to ask if I want go to church. I don't like church, but know it means a lot to her that I go. We drive in my sporty Volkswagen, given to me by my parents for graduation. I still can't believe this car is mine, though I've had it for nearly a year. Mom-mom sits next to me, looking prim, even as I zip recklessly around bends in the Tennessee road.

"Nice little car," she says.

"I still don't believe it's mine."

"It was nice of them to give you such an extravagant gift."

I know she doesn't approve. She doesn't use words like extravagant unless she's expressing disapproval. I don't think she'll believe me, but I try to tell her how I feel.

"I wish they hadn't given it to me. I feel guilty. They spent enough money on my education, and then, when I feel like I owe them something, they give me this car."

"You don't owe them anything."

"Well, I suppose I owe them my success, and I haven't been working too hard on achieving that."

"No one said you had to get a cushy job, just yet. There are worse ways than waitressing to earn a paycheck."

I consider telling her about the pregnancy. She would be happy. She comes from a time when being a mother was the only success a woman needed.

"I don't see why children want to give so much back to their parents," she says. "It's the parents' job to do the giving. Children do the receiving, and when they grow up to be parents, they give to their children. That's the simplicity of it. But people always want to make things complicated."

Her words stir the uncertainty within me. Can I learn the selflessness required for parenting? It's another thing to attend to in the short months ahead.

"Just don't end up like your Pop-pop, please."

"He's sad, I think."

"He doesn't do a thing with himself. It really gets me that he won't even come to church. He's got two legs. He's perfectly capable."

"You two are very different," I say.

"He's so aggravating!" Her voice becomes high-pitched and I look at her. "He's hopeless," she says, and from her pocketbook she pulls a flimsy flowered hanky that old women always seem to carry. I glance at that hanky, and at this moment it's hard to feel for her. It's hard to feel for someone who has done everything right, who has been perpetually prepared. I usually feel sympathy for her, because she tries hard to live an interesting life and she's saddled with someone content to do nothing. But suddenly I'm tired of her endless yearning for his self-improvement.

Maybe it's because the tables are turning, because I won't be the success my family expected, but today I'm siding with the Navy boys and Pop-pops of the world — the people who aren't constantly trying to prove themselves. I wonder if every relationship has a weaker character, and if I'm going to adapt easily to the role.

My grandmother collects herself and we go into the church. I don't listen to the sermon. I'm watching the baby in front of me. She's propped over her mother's shoulder. A pink ribbon gathers most of her hair into a solitary curl. She watches me intently. At first this is nice, but it starts to make me nervous. I run out of silly faces and big smiles. The baby and I look at each other with no expression. I have this creeping feeling she knows a pregnant woman when she sees one. "Don't worry," I want to tell her, "I'm keeping this one." The young mother doesn't stay for Sunday school. She leaves after the sermon. She turns her baby away from me as she gets up. The baby struggles against her mother, works herself around so that she can see me again.

We gather ourselves together and get ready for Sunday school. I feel tired from looking at that baby. I wish I was at the pool instead.

Mom-mom leads the women's Sunday school class. She's patient with the women, who are either very old or very ignorant. Her eyes look upon them with a mixture of exasperation and pity. I wonder if she feels the sin of pride. I know she's guilty of it.

Driving home she says, "I like to think Pop-pop will get to heaven by osmosis."

I'm back at the community pool and so are the teenagers. The sun feels nice on my stomach, which I'm looking at with my critical eye. I'm showing a little bit, but I've always been chunky around the middle. Too much beer in college has left me with a lumpy belly. I'm too lazy to do sit ups. Anyway, now that I'm pregnant, what would be the point?

Mo hasn't called me in many days. I wonder if he's worried, if he's fighting the urge to call. Or maybe he's been busy with his high-powered job. I'm not sure I could tell him I've learned anything at all. It's probably best that he hasn't called.

There's a sound next to me and I open my eyes. It's the girl with the wild hair. She's sitting on her towel, rubbing oil over her chubby arm.

"You won't tell the lifeguard, will you? We're not supposed to wear oil here. It comes off in the water. But I don't plan on swimming anymore, and I like the way it looks."

I smile at her, and she smiles back. She has a beautiful face.

"You're always here," she says. "But before the summer started, I'd never seen you before."

"I'm visiting my grandparents."

"How old are you?"

She's bold. I like her. "I'm twenty-two."

"Do you have a boyfriend?"

"Yes. Do you?"

"Sort of," she says, and looks across the pool at the simple-faced blond boy.

"Together forever?"

"What?" She is disgusted. "I'd never marry any boy from this town. They're all inbreds."

The pool is on top of a small hill. We look across the town toward the Smokies, ancient and purple. She speaks up again and I notice her accent, lightly Southern.

"My mother's from Detroit. I was born there, but I don't remember anything except this town. As soon as I'm old enough, I'll go back to Detroit."

"How old are you?"

"Fifteen." She says it like a challenge, like I might want to do something about it.

"What if something happened to disturb your plans? What if you got pregnant?"

"I'd have an abortion," she says, still looking at the mountains. "I'm not worried about that though. You'd be seriously insane to get too involved with one of these rednecks."

"Come on," I laugh. "They can't all be bad!"

"Well, there's one who's OK," she says, nodding toward the group of boys, and though I can't tell which one she's singling out, I'm sure it's not the blond.

"I'm pregnant," I tell her. She's the first person to know besides Mo.

She looks at me and her face lights up. "Really? Oh, neat. See, I like kids. I don't mean to sound like I don't. If I got pregnant now, I'd have an abortion. But if I was twenty-two, I'd be happy."

"Twenty-two isn't that old."

"Yeah, I know. But I'd be ready. I already know exactly what I want to do. I won't be wasting time figuring out my career. I'm going to be a midwife."

"A midwife?" It seems like a strange coincidence, given all our pregnancy talk.

"Yeah, midwives are making a big comeback. They're like doctors, but they specialize only in pregnancies. You don't have to go to school quite as long as doctors."

"Oh."

"I read a lot. I know a lot about it. I could probably help you have your baby at this point." She looks right at me.

"Well, I'll have to go back to the father soon."

"Are you married?"

"No. But in love."

"Oh, that's great."

We watch the boys. Their tanned bodies look like television images superimposed on the backdrop of the Smokies. They are laughing, hands lightly brushing the ripples of their own stomachs. I decide that I'd touch my stomach a lot too, if it looked like any of those.

"So," she says, "you came to see your grandparents."

"Yes, that's right."

"Why don't you visit your mother, if you're trying to figure out parenthood?"

"My mom's really busy all the time, and I just wanted to relax — no questions, no pressure. My grandparents have more time to talk, I guess."

"You don't like your mother much?"

"Of course I do. But she really expects success, which stresses me out sometimes. It makes me wonder how my child will feel about me."

"Don't drive yourself crazy. Your children will never like you. You just have to do your job."

She's such an adult. I love this girl. I wish she was my teenager. "You don't like your mother?"

"She's alright. She did an amazing thing, you know, bringing me into the world. I just think it's amazing. But, we're all different people. We don't choose each other. We're thrown together. Like, if I could choose a mom, I'd choose somebody like you."

"You would?" I ask, feeling flattered but at the same time not trusting her. Then I remember that this is how most adults must feel around her.

"Oh, I like you," she says. "You're easy to talk to. You treat me like a normal person. Some people are lucky. They get really cool moms. My friend Ashley, her mom smokes pot with her. That's cool."

"Your mom's not very cool?"

"She does her job. That's all I can ask. I'm not complaining. Not too much."

"Maura!" A girl from the crowd of teenagers waves my friend over. "Maura, what're you doing?"

"That's Ashley. We're going in the woods back there to smoke some pot. Do you want to come?"

I feel myself blushing. I haven't smoked pot since I was seventeen. "No. The baby."

"Oh, right. Well, why not just come along? Hang out?"

I've been watching these kids for so many days now, it seems rude not to join them. I stand and wrap my towel around my hips in a kind of sarong. "Let's go," I say.

The concrete is rough and hot on my heels and I hope introductions won't take too long. Of course, they don't. Teenagers are so casual. I've forgotten.

Then we're walking past the tall fence enclosing the pool and up a hill into a wooded area. We walk about a quarter of a mile on an overgrown path, and I'm a little angry at the kids for not reminding me to bring shoes. They're all wearing flip-flops, immune to the small sticks and pieces of glass I have to watch for.

We come to a clearing. The kids have set up a hang-out area, with car seats and old living room chairs arranged in a circle. I can hear the sound of Route 66 not too far away, but I can't see it. We're well hidden.

The kids spread themselves out on the furniture. I pick a bar stool and immediately regret it: I'm perched at least a foot higher than all of them. The joint gets lit by Maura's boyfriend. He exhales and begins laughing and coughing loudly. His face turns bright red. "Gimme that," Maura says, rolling her eyes. She grabs the joint and takes a hit, passes it to Ashley before she exhales, and when she exhales, her lips are full and beautiful, the smoke billows above her like the thinnest, most fluid silk.

Ashley takes a hit and passes the joint to her boyfriend, who holds it too long. The boy next to Ashley's boyfriend is tall and tan, with dirty blond hair and the most perfect nipples I've ever seen, the size of quarters, smooth and round, the color of almonds. He takes his hit and I am nervous, because he'll be passing it to me next, and before I can object he is standing up and bringing it to me. I feel bad because he has gone to trouble for nothing.

"No, I don't. Um, I can't."

He nods, no judgment, and brings the joint over to Maura's boyfriend. Maura's eyes follow the boy with the nipples. It seems that she stares at him in a way that is practiced casual. He's the one she wants, I realize.

The joint gets passed around a few more times, and there isn't much talking, just some gentle laughter; even Maura's awkward boyfriend seems to have calmed down. Then, when the joint is finished, the couples turn to each other and begin kissing, and it's a make-out party.

The boy with the perfect nipples is alone, though. He gets up and walks a few yards away, picks up a stick and crouches down, poking the stick into something in the dirt, an antpile maybe. He looks over his shoulder and sees me watching him. He smiles lazily, stands up and walks over to me. I feel stoned, pulled into the rhythm of the people around me. He stands in front of me. "Want to see some flowers?" he asks, and I resist looking over at Maura making out on the couch. I edge off the stool and begin walking with the boy.

We come to a field and the sudden burst of sunlight surprises me. We seem to have walked for awhile, my feet are coated with dirt. The sound of the highway has diminished and

I realize I have no idea where we are in relation to the pool. The field is overgrown with wild flowers.

"Oh, wow, that's really pretty," I say, leaning against a tree and looking out over the field. Convenient tree, says a voice in my head. And I know my stance is vulnerable, ready. I'm not being very responsible. So I'm thinking about standing up straight, maybe walking away from this boy, but I feel his presence, he's getting closer and I turn my head to face him and we're kissing. His lips are so full and moist and *young*.

He sets his hands on my hips. He steps closer, pushes his hands around my bare back. Just like a boy, his mouth is already opening, so I open mine: a french kiss, smoothness and mint and his thick breathing mixing with mine. It's a long kiss, like they always were at fifteen. As if there were a record that had to be broken.

Then it stops and he leans back and smiles. His eyes are slanted and red. Stoned. "I've been wanting to do that since you first came to the pool," he says. "I've been watching you."

"You have, huh?" I give him a sideways glance, then look down, past our bodies, to the stray flowers at our feet, the ones on the outskirts of the field. I'm being coy. I wish I would stop.

"Yes," he says, and kisses me again. I hadn't been watching him. I'd hardly noticed him until today; I've been busy concentrating on Maura. He pushes his hand up the middle of my back to the nape of my neck. He squeezes the back of my neck just so. Oh, he's very good at this.

Then, what am I doing? What the Hell? I'm practically married, I'm pregnant, this is the boy Maura likes — and this is only a boy!

But, before I stop him, I run my hands over the hairless chest, over his nipples, flat and taut; they break my heart.

But it has to stop, so I push him gently off me.

"Shouldn't we be getting back?" I ask.

"Mmm. OK," he says, disappointed. We walk back to the hang-out, and on the way, he says, "Can I call you?"

I look at him, shocked, and I remember what it was, to be fifteen. The other part, the nervous and vulnerable part, and I feel like dirt. His face is innocent, waiting. "I'm sorry," I say, stammering. "I'm going home soon, I don't think it would be a good idea."

"Oh," he says.

"Look, I didn't know this would be a make-out party," I say. My laugh sounds lame.

"Yeah," he laughs too, an artificial laugh.

We get to the clearing and the others are waiting. "We were getting ready to go, you guys," says Maura. She seems angry, which gives me a strange, almost gleeful sensation.

"Shit. I'm supposed to mow the lawn before dark," her boyfriend says.

"Were we gone that long?" I ask.

Maura shrugs. "Well," she says, smirking and tilting her head, "long enough."

We get back to the pool and the boy kisses me so suddenly, in front of everyone, embarrassing me. I see Maura out of the corner of my eye. She's glaring. She's angry. Good, I think, and immediately wish I hadn't thought it. It's possible that I've been competing with Maura, that I've been trying to knock this fifteen-year-old down a notch. Because she's at the top of her game, because she's as confident as I was at her age.

"Good-bye," the boy says.

"Good-bye," I say, and then I call, "Good-bye!" to Maura, but she is walking away already, pretending not to hear me.

I turn back toward my things at the far side of the pool, then stop and turn toward the water instead. I dive into the pool, feel the water like fingers peeling something from my skin. My lips still tingle from that boy's lips and I know I've failed to progress. I'm a selfish person, jealous of a life I can no longer have.

I dislike my past self, who disdained simple boys, who made ruthless decisions, but this older me, who acts passive and spiteful, is no bargain either.

Emerged from the water, I am no less anxious, no more cleansed.

I call information for a long time, trying to find the parents of José. The computer only gives two numbers at a time, and there are dozens of José Perezes in the directory. I find his mother finally. She wants to know how I am; she liked me very much. José is married and living in Hialeah, near the race track. He works construction. He has a little boy, named Jesus. He's happy. She wishes me well, hopes I'm doing well. She gives me his number.

I call the number and my hand is shaking. What will I possibly say? The door to the room is closed. Soon Mom-mom will call me to dinner. I'll sit next to Pop-pop who'll breathe heavily and won't look up from his food.

There are two rings. "Hello?" José's wife has a heavy Cuban accent. I hear the boy crying in the background. It's a strong, healthy cry.

"Hello? Is José there?" I say, and take a deep breath. She has already put the phone down, is already calling him to the phone.

But what will I say? I have come down to earth. I'm sorry I was such a snot back then and I'm sorry it took me until now to realize how awful I was. I'm not the success I thought I would be. After today, I'm no longer that teenager you knew, thank God.

There is nothing to say.

"Yeah?" José asks.

I hang up right away.

What a fool I am. How can it take seven years to learn remorse? And why should José want to hear about it now?

The right thing to do would be to call my parents and give them the news, commit to my new life by announcing it. You'll be grandparents, I'll say. Maybe this is how I'll repay you, by learning the selflessness of parenthood. I hope I can learn to be a grown-up.

I lay back on the bed and put my hands over my eyes. I feel a flutter—the first time I have sensed the baby.
The phone rings and it's Mo. How do I feel? Humbled. I hope I feel humbled. Will I be coming home? Yes, I'm coming home. He wants to know what's wrong with my voice. Have I been crying? I'm thinking about the other baby, I tell him. The one I didn't have. Oh, he says, and his tone sounds like he's stumped, at a loss for words. I felt the baby, just now, almost like a kick, more like a tickle, I tell him. I hope he likes his mother, Mo. I hope he can forgive me for the way I am, for the way I've lived.

Make it Good

Tommy squirmed with the two remaining contestants on the outdoor stage. His hair was pulled and tugged into desperate, spiky black tufts that framed his face, more red than I'd ever seen it. He had purposely held his bladder for most of a day and was about to burst. Of course I thought he looked adorable.

In all our years together at Blatherton Public Relations, ranked the fifteenth largest firm of its kind in Chicago, Tommy had shown me many times that he was a wait-till-the-last-minute type. It was his defining quality, and as much as it drove me nuts, it drove me love-crazy too.

This was the third "Hold It" contest for our client, Contingent Comfortgarments. *Because Confidence is Contingent on Comfort.* People entered for the chance to win a free trip to Puerto Rico ("Explore the waterfalls of the rainforest!"), but the publicity, though plentiful, sometimes focused on the urinary dangers of the contest. I begged Tommy not to do it again this year, but he was a fool for endurance exercises.

INVENTING VICTOR

I stood in the audience, talking to my sister Sally on my cell phone. It was the same old topic. I wanted Tommy to marry me.

"Why won't he marry me?" I said into the cell.

"Ugh," said Sally, a born-again living in the Deep South. "Don't rush it. Once you're married, you have to be submissive."

"Well, no I don't."

"Oh, sure. It's written."

"Right, but so is this." I read to her off a brochure from that afternoon's press check. "'When picnicking, pack canned foods in your cooler. You won't have to worry about bruising those delicious canned peaches.'" I shoved it back into my bag and almost dropped the phone.

"Is that the word of God?" she was saying.

"No. I wrote it."

"And it's pretty good. On the human scale."

"I'll never get your Christian crap about being submissive, Sally."

"It's simple. By being submissive, you show your husband what it is to be submissive to God. You teach by example."

"Ooh, the band stopped," I said to Sally. Nu Shooz had finished playing their ancient hit "I Can't Wait."

"Tommy will say something in a minute," I said, giving Sally the play-by-play.

"He's ruining his male organs by holding it so long," Sally said.

I stared at Tommy. He was in the exact pose you would expect from someone holding it. "I'm hanging in there!" he said into the mike.

"He uses the wrong kind of bicycle seat too," I said to Sally. "We're doomed for a sterile landscape."

Sally had four children and was pregnant again. I told her she was exceeding the population control limit for both of us. If our family was going to maintain zero population growth, I said, she had already ruled out my chances for parenting. And now, with a fifth on the way, she'd have to kill a family member to even the scales.

"Well, and you," she went on. "Waiting till past thirty to bear young is terrible for your uterus. Not to mention that damn pill you're taking. So harmful to your reproductive system."

"Every other system can go to hell, Sally. The ecosystem. The political system. The monetary system. But heaven forbid anything should happen to the precious reproductive system."

"I'm sick of this systematic abuse," she said. "Listen, I am good at reproducing. It's a talent. So, why stop?"

My nephew wailed in the background. "Gotta go," Sally said. "God bless."

Being with Tommy was always fun – and I was good at it. Lots of wrestling and dancing and kissing and playing around. Everyone saw how great we were together. But still, it had taken him two years of dating before he would say he loved me.

"I love this place," he had said about a year ago at the Blatherton offices, leaning his cute frame on my cubicle wall. "Isn't it awesome to touch the untouchable?" he continued. "No one else would have the balls to get this creative."

We had just had the video thumbnails approved for the *Asparagus, The Funky Tinkle* campaign.

With Contingent as our biggest account, none of us in the office could think about anything but pee. Amazingly, the Asparagus Commission liked our idea (*Can YOU Do the Funky Tinkle?)*, probably because the campaign was *working*. Apparently some people weren't aware of the smelly affect asparagus has on most urine, and were buying up the veggie just to see if they were in the 70-percent club.

"I just love it here!" Tommy flopped onto my guest chair—as lanky and adorable as I could ever dream a boy to be, playing with the wind-up rutabaga on my desk.

"I knew when you came here you were Blatherton material," I said, stalling, not one to savor the confrontation I had planned. But I needed to shake him up. How could he love this place so much and not admit to loving me? I mean, I liked parts of my job, but not like he did. The mischievous side of me was titillated by getting people to act on things they shouldn't care about, but mostly it made me feel shitty. And I hated people for buying into it. We all made fun of the consumers. The internal Blatherton asparagus sales-mapping charts featured a cartoon guy on the toilet, an elated look on his face as he savored the fumes rising from his pee.

But really, what sheep — buying more asparagus just because TV said: *smell your pee!* When would they rebel? Deep down, I hoped a campaign would fail, that consumers would prove they were independent thinkers.

Tommy never saw a down side to Blatherton and so I kept my opinions to myself. Instead I schemed about getting out, then agonized that leaving the firm could mean losing contact with Tommy.

"It's been great," Tommy oozed. "You've been great." He gave me that deep look I'd seen him use on clients at a big pitch.

"Yeah. And, Tommers. It's been two years."

"No no. Three years. Three years and four months."

"Not since you've been at Blatherton! Two years since we've been — well." Oh, why did I bother? "Whatever we are." I swiveled away from him.

"Meg, not this again!" He jumped up and hugged me from behind. The back of my chair separated us like a stodgy chaperone. He kissed me again and again on my neck and shoulders. I pointed and clicked on the dancing rutabaga at the American Vegetable Association website. Maybe I was like a rutabaga. So good for him that he didn't want me. I would need a whole PR campaign to get him to *love* me.

"No." I wheeled back and maybe nipped his toe. "That's it. I love you. I have said that more than one hundred times and you have never answered." I looked right into those sky-blue eyes. "I can't do it alone. I can't love alone." I stood and slammed my hand on the wind up toy, feeling it squirm under my palm.

Tommy looked a tad hurt. He swept the chair away and grasped me movie style, dip and all—planted a really lovely one.

I recovered, patting my lips primly and turning to shut down the computer.

"It's over," I said.

He let it lie for a whole week. I spent every alone minute crying. When I saw him in the halls I darted into other people's cubes and pretended to talk to them. I sent out some resumes to other agencies and in-house PR departments, but found myself frantic at the thought of leaving Tommy. If I couldn't really have him, I whined to myself, I could at least still work with him. I could still participate in brainstorms with him or pull a few all-nighters working on a big pitch.

On the seventh day, lo, as Sally would say, there was a note on my desk. No flowers, just a simple note. "Of course I love you. But my core competency is word cheapening. With you, I use sparingly, because it's the real McCoy."

How easily I forgave. It's hard to be so crazy about someone.

But then he wouldn't move in together and I had to threaten again. He didn't want to meet my parents. Shopping together for clothes and furniture made him "feel funny." He thought a one-week vacation to the Riviera was "getting a little too entrenched." Entrenched? I had calluses from putting my foot down so often. My colleagues joked at lunch, naming me Tatum Ultimatum. But he came through each time, better late than never.

The sky was darkening and poor Tommy hadn't peed since six in the morning. I checked my watch and started to wander around in the thickening crowd.

I spotted the marketing director for our co-sponsor, In-Loo-Of mobile latrines. He waved and I wiggled my fingers in the corporate-mandated pantomime of e-mailing ("Whenever you report on correspondence, wiggle your fingers like it all happened over e-mail," our boss boomed at a staff meeting. "It's how we establish ourselves as the e-agency.") I mouthed the words, "I'll e-mail you," and turned tail, ducking into another gaggle of event-watchers. I wasn't planning on fielding any complaints from clients. Not to be bitter, but who gave a crap? So much work—months of planning—for a stupid event about undergarments. Please. There had to be something more fulfilling in life.

At least on the weekends Tommy and I could be together, sans Blatherton—whooping and hollering as we disposed of our incomes and romped around town together. After three years, he still gave me the butterflies. Even living in the same apartment with him couldn't relieve me of my girlish crush. I would turn and hit the snooze and think about going back to sleep and then realize the bed was so *warm*, realizing he was right there and all I had to do was roll over and hug him. His stillness under the covers was pure bliss. But Tommy never stayed put for long. He loved to jump out of bed and get dressed for another day at his dream job.

As I walked among the snickering audience members, I looked up at the buildings, admiring the illusion my changing perspective created: their walls like gleaming masts of giant ships gliding through the clouds.

I had to get free of Blatherton, but before I left, I had to be secure that Tommy was mine. Surely he knew what fun it would be for two star event planners to plan a wedding. I had to plan a wedding before I hit thirty-five, I realized, if only because I would be so darn good at it.

"I can't take it anymore!" Tommy cried into the mike, running off stage. The emcee threw his hands in the air and laughed. The two remaining contestants grimaced and bobbed in their internal liquid.

And that's when I had the big idea: *Meg-n-Tommy Mania*, a brand-building event in honor of our love.

I figured I could end up making back my expenses through the plate charge of $200 per person and could still give proceeds to the local unwed mothers assistance fund. So this was no frivolous affair. If a corporation can do it, so can a union. Even if it's just a union of two people. Even if we weren't quite joined yet.

Tommy didn't object when I first told him about my plans. His only comment was, "Isn't that putting the cart before the horse?" I emphasized many times that it was absolutely not an engagement party. Just a celebration, I said.

Meg-n-Tommy Mania would be a black tie affair, attended by friends and colleagues mostly, with a sprinkling of people earnest about the unwed mothers cause. Tommy contributed to some of the planning. He helped pick the band and the venue. He sat at the coffee table many nights addressing the invitations in his pristine script.

"Now, tell me what our guests are getting out of this again? What pain points are we addressing?" he called to me one night from his stacks of envelopes and cards. I was in the kitchen testing out hors d'oeuvre recipes.

"They're contributing to the unwed mothers' cause, and they're getting to know Meg-n-Tommy better than they ever have before."

"I see a lot of these people every day, you know?" he said. "They know we're a good couple. Why all this extra emphasis?"

I sighed, although I was glad Tommy hadn't realized the event was more for him than the guests. "I just want to throw a fun party! Our relationship is as good a reason as any. Better than most, really, don't you think? At Blatherton we waste our time planning events for jock itch powder, gas relief medicine and motor oil!"

"That's not a waste, Meg. That's money in the bank, which means jobs for hard-working Americans. That's to increase sales for our clients. To attract new consumers," he said.

He wasn't being belligerent, just thorough. Tommy was known for continually tweaking a campaign.

"Now, which new consumers need to buy into Meg-n-Tommy?" he asked.

YOU! I wanted to yell, but a cardinal rule of pushing product is keeping the sales pitch subtle.

"You're trying to read too much into it," I said. "I want to throw a party because I want the whole world to know I love you and because I want to raise some money for a good cause." I walked over to him with a crab puff and popped it into his mouth.

"Mmm," he smiled and swallowed. "I invited the Asparagus Commission people. Make sure you add asparagus to these. Oh, and don't forget to serve Fizzy Beer. We need to keep them happy with Blatherton after that bad headline they got last month."

"'Extra Bubbles Cause Cramping?'"

"Right," Tommy said, pulling me down for a crab-sweet smooch.

The taste of his lips fresh on mine, I flopped down on the couch and wished I could relax for a week or ten. But, I knew Tommy liked to see me campaigning. I knew he liked the productivity of our little project. It would be worth it, I hoped, and I saved my biggest smiles for him.

Looking up at the ceiling, listening to Tommy's calligraphy pen softly scratch the parchment, I rationalized, and it all made sense. With the marriage, I could feel secure about letting Tommy go to Blatherton without me each day. But without marriage, there was that gnawing sensation that Blatherton would win.

Sally took this opportunity to visit, leaving the kids with her husband. "I'm dying to see what has Tommy so hot and bothered all the time," she said, referring to Blatherton events. I promised her it would be great, but as the days crept up on me, as I lost more sleep over the planning, I became more and more uneasy.

The afternoon of the big event Sally and I were at the mirror getting ready. Tommy was already at the site, meeting with the caterers and going over the band's play list. I looked at my big sister and wanted to tell her how tired I was. Exhausted from all the little details, all the snotty people whose asses I'd had to kiss to pull this thing off. I wanted to hug her and cry.

"You know, I'm afraid I've made a bigger deal about this than I should have," I said, watching Sally struggle with her fake eyelashes. "I guess it's my PR nature anymore, to make a big deal about stuff."

She laughed. "Do you have cold feet?"

"No, I just. You know, unwed mothers. They're not very godly. You won't like it."

"He who is without sin casts the first stone! You need a drink," she said. She whisked out of the bathroom and returned in minutes with rum and cokes for both of us.

"Sally, what about the baby?"

"At this point the baby's fully formed. And it's just a little nip," she smiled. "Bottoms up!"

Sally's presence, despite her holiday demeanor, made things worse. Suddenly I was embarrassed by my event. By the time we had a full house that night, I was in a panic. Wasn't there a legal limit on sequins? The ice sculpture seemed lubricated and obscene. And the cigarette girls: whose idea was that? At midnight, live doves would drop from the ceiling. That was a little much, but how could I cancel it now? Where the hell was the Romanian dove trainer? Probably smoking pot out back with the dishwashers.

"Pretty fancy, huh?" I asked Sally.

She seemed impressed, but I had that uneasy sensation, watching all of these same people, together at another event. I knew none of the attendees cared that I couldn't get Tommy to concentrate on our love for one Blatherton minute. But still they had dropped hundreds of dollars a plate.

"I'll never forget when Tommy first told me he was dating Meg," our director, Cyril Blatherton, was saying into the mike. I stood in the back with Sally by the punch bowl but somehow Blatherton managed to see me and wink. "Tommy did it over e-mail, because I was away in Hong Kong at the time.

"'Mr. Blatherton,' wrote Tommy." Blatherton air-typed lavishly. "'I am now dating Meg Flanagan. We felt it was best to alert you to the matter, since we are not sure of the company's policy on inter-office dating.'

"'Goshdarnit, Morgan,' I replied." Blatherton's fingers punched the air like a concert pianist's. "'Read your employment manual! At Blatherton, we encourage inter-office dating. It increases the likelihood that employees will stay at work later and longer!'"

The crowd laughed, pairs turning to each other to nod at the clever business sense. Tommy sidled up to me then, whispering in my ear, "I think I just sealed the new Fizzy deal."

I smiled at him through my uneasiness. I examined his profile but couldn't gauge the effect of all this brand-building. I wondered if Tommy was as convinced of our relationship as everyone else.

I had the distinct feeling that it was all a mistake. I had planned this event because I knew how, but that wasn't reason enough. I wondered if there were creatures in the world that hated doing what came naturally. Spiders who hated weaving webs, beavers who hated building dams, birds who hated to fly.

"Mr. Blatherton's funny!" Sally cried. "What a nice boss."

I rolled my eyes and tried to remember how many times I'd seen her fill her punch glass.

"So, all my best to a wonderful pair," Blatherton continued. "And I want to commend Meg on pulling off a fabulous party."

Then the unwed mother gave her speech about going back to college to follow her dream of accounting. I zoned out, leaning my head against Tommy's lapel, taking in the odor of his cologne. Was he sold? Would he be brand loyal? Did I care anymore?

I had spent most of my career despising the people I was trying to sell. If Tommy bought into my scheme, how would he be any different from them? A woman daubing her handkerchief to her eye caught my attention and I realized that half the room was misty from the unwed mother's speech.

"Very moving," Tommy whispered, kissing my hair. "You must have written her speech," he said.

"Damn, Tommy," I said. "Just because it gets an emotional response doesn't mean it's been fabricated."

"Accounting, huh?" Sally said loudly, so that the crowd turned back and looked at her. She started shoving people aside, moving through the crowd before I could stop her. "Listen, I'm Meg's sister, and I don't think I'm on the docket, but if you wouldn't mind, I'd like to say a word or two."

The unwed mother leaned into the mike and said softly, "Well, I was wrapping up, so um, thank you everyone, thank you so much."

Sally was already up onstage.

"I'm a Christian," she said, and the mike squealed with feedback. "And as a Christian, I'm not a big fan of women working. Children are our greatest treasure and it's a privilege to be responsible for raising them. But that's not what I want to say," she leaned into the podium, practically stretched out over it.

"Where's crisis management?" Tommy whispered harshly, squeezing my arm and stalking away. I stood frozen, wondering what my sister would do next.

"What I want to say is that accounting is great," she said, "but to all you unwed mothers: don't go into public relations. My little sister spends twenty-four hours a day trying to convince people of things she usually doesn't believe in herself. And even when she does seem to believe in it—like with this event, for example—it's too much darn work! Bless her heart—she'll find her way once the Lord sees to it, I know she will. So, here's to any career direction but the one my li'l sister Meg chose," she held up her glass, surveyed the room of people who wouldn't toast with her, and then tossed back the rest of her punch. She took a deep breath and leaned into the mike again, ready for round two of her speech.

Suddenly, Tommy was onstage, taking Sally by the arm and moving her away from the mike. "Thanks, Sally," he said with a gentle laugh, passing her off to the crisis management usher who stood behind him. "I'm sure Mr. Blatherton appreciates that frank career advice. But, uh, I'm up here to say that, um, I love PR and I think I've finally met someone who's better at it than me."

I watched the usher escort Sally offstage—visibly pregnant woman drunk at my event. Indeed what we would call a crisis. Tommy was probably fuming and Sally was probably being taken to the containment room for a little cool-off session. I stood there, not sure what to do, then realized all faces were turned to me.

Tommy was gazing at me in that strange, solemn way. He took the mike off its stand, stepped out from behind the podium and then fell to his knees. "You've outdone yourself, honeypie," he said. The crowd gasped; it quivered like a big bowl of jelly.

"This event," he continued. "All of these people. You've convinced me. I'm a believer, Meg. I'm sold American. Will you marry me?"

People were clapping. I heard women crying joyful tears. I had no idea what I was feeling. Something like dismay. Or doom. I couldn't read Tommy's face. It was a mask. Maybe it always had been. The crowd quieted, seemed to hold its collective breath.

I decided that there were two possible motivations for Tommy's proposal. Either he was truly convinced by my campaigning, in which case he reminded me of the little character on the toilet smelling his pee—who I could not marry. Or he was diverting attention from my drunk and pregnant sister, putting his entire future on the line for the love of image control, and I couldn't marry someone that calculating either.

I backed away. I backed away through the velvet curtains behind me—away from the crowd of believers enrapt in an empty promise.

I heard a gasp from one elderly man, saw the feather of a lady's hat quivering in the crowd. Just before the curtains swallowed me from their sight forever, I said, "Don't believe just because it sounds good."

I stumbled about for hours on the downtown streets. I had no idea what to do with myself. I worried about Sally alone in the containment room. But I didn't know if I could face her. She had been shamed; whisked away like something dirty.

Sally might make mistakes—public ones—but she was the only one I knew who believed in something that seemed remotely important. At least Sally had God.

It was near midnight when I found myself in a city square, at the center of which stood a massive clock. The only people around were sleeping lumps on park benches.

The clock face glowed at me, wise and alone. And I wondered who was the public relations practitioner for the Truth in all its fullness and beauty. And why was he so silent? But then maybe I just couldn't hear it, couldn't see whatever truth was right in front of me. Maybe I was like Tommy, who was like the rest of us: waiting for someone to make it good. Give me that sign. Take my short attention span into account. Make it flashy. Make it pretty and I might buy.

I couldn't make it good anymore. Not for anybody, but especially not for someone who was as in love with making it good as Tommy was. Tommy loved Blatherton and I hated it. Nothing about our union would change that. It was the fact of our relationship that I had failed to fully recognize. How I had let it go on so long I wasn't sure. Maybe because I had always been successful with my work. But that was no excuse for sticking with it anymore.

I wondered if Sally would let me come live with her in the South, spend time with her children, greet the new baby, and straighten myself out. I didn't need to plan a wedding with Tommy. I needed to plan an escape. Better yet, I needed to escape without a plan.

And there was a rush of hope just for me, washing over me, when I acknowledged that I was no bird or spider stuck in some instinctual role, but I was capable of change. I could drop this skill—in fact, call it a curse—and be someone totally different. From here on, if I was going to make it good it wasn't going to be about products, events or executive boys. I didn't know what it would be for, but it would be for something real.

Comfort Isn't Everything

JENNIFER BANNAN

Piotr threw aside the sign with my name on it, took my face in his large hands and kissed me. "Wait," I cried, dropping my bags, pulling at the strap that cut into my shoulder. We laughed and kissed as the bags fell around us like a flower opening. His full lips felt like a delicious memory, like I had kissed him thousands of times already. It seemed less like a vacation and more like coming home – to be in Russia with Piotr. Here were the colorless hallways of Krasnodar Airport, directing us down escalators that led to more drab hallways. Here was the language I barely knew, the increased presence of headcoverings and body odor, and all of it washing me with the "ah, yes" sensation of recognition. For here was Piotr, who to this point I had only physically known as backlit letters on the screen, but who had moved me more than any man yet, even Tolstoy.

"You are more lovely than your JPEGs," he laughed. We grinned at our strange fate. We felt shy, embarrassed by our trendiness. We felt foolish to have met over the Internet. Yet we were overwhelmed by the romance of it.

At baggage claim, Piotr shifted feet as I grabbed bag after bag from the conveyor belt. His tiny smiles betrayed his discomfort over the amount of luggage I had brought. Since I was altogether unsure of Russian styles and weather, I had packed a sampling of everything.

"Did you stockings for my mother and aunts? The kind fit for Queens?" he asked.

"Yes, they're in here," I said, laughing and patting one of my trunks. His eyes brightened and he placed a hand on my hair.

At his apartment, my trunks took up a terrible portion of the bedroom. I propped them on end and stacked his books and shoes on them. "You really need a nightstand on this side," I said, and placed another trunk vertically beside the bed. Problem solved.

I pointed at the desk with his computer. It partially blocked his open closet. "Is this where we met?" I asked. I had pictured him typing to me, while looking out a window at onion domes, smoking clove cigarettes. But all the while he had been gazing into his closet of hanging clothes. There were no windows in his bedroom.

He grinned. "Where I fell in love," he said.

I took the two steps across the room to the desk and the ancient computer sitting on it. No wonder it had taken so long for him to respond during our chats. This computer had no power. So many times I had paced my own apartment floor, worrying over what he would say to my outlandish declarations of love. I had been in the middle of *Anna Karenina*. Piotr was my Vronsky, childish and petulant but so tempting, so charming. I didn't think I was selfish like Anna, and I wasn't married like Anna, but I believed I was as passionate as she. And as impulsive as Anna, making the trip here, knowing without question it was love.

He popped open a trunk and found the stockings among my other things. "Michelle," he said with dismay. "They will need these stockings for the next few years until someone else visits from the West. And from what I understand, they tear easily!" He opened the packaging and pulled out the hose, pushing his hand into the tube of fabric, so that his arm hair flattened.

"They don't tear. They run."

"Well, maybe when the lady wearing them is running," he said.

"No, 'run' is how you describe it," I said, laughing again. "Never mind! I thought fifteen pairs was a lot."

"That's barely two each," he said.

"Well, Piotr, you're a chemist," I teased, twisting the panty hose around his neck. "Make some nylon in the lab. Start a business that will make you rich." I pushed him onto the bed, yanking on his belt and straddling him.

He laughed and said, "I feel as though I'll be eaten alive."

My days in his apartment were long but not unpleasant. I stayed away from the computer, which, now that I was with Piotr in person, reminded me too much of work. I wrote letters to my family and friends, read long novels, and tried to write in a journal about my observations of Russia. I dreaded answering the phone, for my mother was often on the other end, worrying about the international news, which she had just begun to follow for the first time in her life, and only because I was here in Russia.

"It's just that things are so much more desperate outside of the United States," she said.

"Oh, not really. People seem pretty well adapted to life here," I said.

"Well, those people have never known stability in the way you've known it. They'll adapt to anything. The governments are very unstable, darling. Anything can happen in that kind of environment."

I assured her that all seemed calm from where I stood, and I hung up, sure she would continue her open worrying with my father.

Each morning Piotr asked, "What will you do today?" while running water into a bucket and setting it aside for tea. Water service was shut off from noon till five. I had discovered the night before that it was also shut from midnight until five in the morning, when I woke for a glass of water and turned the faucet, only to be shocked fully awake by the hacking, wheezing clank of the struggling pipes.

"I'll sit around today and relax. I don't know."

"So, you'll 'play it by ear'?" he asked, testing out his English on the cliche.

"Yes."

"I don't know how you can stand it! If you have no plans, how can you fit me into your future?"

"Oh, don't you worry," I teased. "My plans for you are big and exciting."

But Piotr was right. I wasn't much of a planner. I didn't intend to think about any aspirations during this trip. All I knew was that I had four more weeks of this complete freedom from responsibility. My job had been keeping me busy racing market competitors for seven years straight—and my brand was the winner in its category of anti-smoking gum. This was my first real vacation. I felt entitled to it.

"When resources are limited as they are in Russia, people make planning a big part of the day," Piotr said.

Piotr worked in a lab where he lacked many of the tools or chemicals he needed. He said he managed to get work done with his limited resources, but there were research questions he was prevented from exploring. He dreamed of coming to America to study but then admitted that he could never leave the country and people he loved.

"Planning in America means lots of big meetings around shiny conference tables and fancy breakfast treats," I said. "A waste of dollars, really."

He shook his head, laughing and pulling on his jacket. By the time he was gone I realized I had forgotten to ask him for better directions to the grocery store. It was difficult to find groceries in Piotr's town and I had already asked about them several times. He was speaking to me mostly in Russian — my request — and his directions were vague and confusing and I would invariably get lost walking, my stomach growling.

Piotr was generous with everything but the food. He read to me as I bathed in the tub. His reading voice was resonant and full in the tiny bathroom. He rubbed my feet and washed my hair, telling me stories of his childhood.

And he listened as well as he talked. He pulled stories out of me I had forgotten, about the small struggles I had had with parents over boyfriends, the humiliating time my college roommates had stolen my clothes, and the time I was passed up for promotion at work by a younger, pushy colleague. He wanted to know more about my past, but at times I felt there was no sense going back over it, since there had been nothing truly difficult to overcome, no real sacrifices to make. Piotr had lived through hunger, through the war with Afghanistan, his brother's death there as a soldier, and the loss of his father to cancer. His were real struggles, and mine seemed superficial in comparison.

I had a hunch Piotr was eating plenty at work. Often his collar smelled of wonderful fried onions and potatoes.

"Here's some ice cream," he said one afternoon upon arriving home. "Americans always eat it, don't they?"

I was famished and made myself a dish. It was Neapolitan, not my favorite kind, and too soft. "Would you like some?" I asked, sitting on the couch next to him with my legs curled under me.

He shook his head with what seemed like impatience.

"What are we doing tonight?" I asked.

"You constantly want to be *entertained.* You never stay still." He grabbed my hip and pulled at the flesh. I dipped my spoon into the soft ice cream. Perhaps Piotr thought I was fat. I had looked through old pictures and seen good looking, thin Russian girlfriends.

He pulled at the waistband of my skirt, dipped his head and kissed my stomach.

"I gave you ideas for things we could do and you said I wasn't being spontaneous," he said.

"Well, you wanted immediate commitment. You wanted me to pick a time on the clock before I had decided if it sounded fun."

He pushed up behind me on the couch and pulled my chin around to kiss my lips. "Mmm. Sticky."

I took one last bite from the cold spoon and then set my dish aside. "What do you do all day?" I asked, pulling at his lapel. "All day in the lab, are you making delicious lunches?"

"Oh, you'd like to know, wouldn't you?" he asked, pulling off my blouse in three rough tugs.

I slid onto the floor, onto my knees, told him in the States we eat tubesteak.

He laughed, let his head fall back as I took him in my mouth.

"Enough," he said after a minute. He pushed me back onto the floor, struggling the rest of the way out of his pants, stripping off mine.

"Tonight I'm having you for dinner," he said. "Instead of the other way around."

He was rough, a brat, smacking and yanking and threatening to come. "I won't wait for you, because I'm selfish," he whispered in my ear as he pounded.

I came immediately.

"You didn't!" he said, lifting away from me, his face amazed.

I nodded and grinned. "Come on," I said, urging him on.

"How is it you always get what you want? Spoiled American girl." He relaxed and kissed me, leaned into me, sighing.

"Don't you want to finish?" I asked. I felt his shrug press into my shoulder and for a moment I dozed.

Piotr stood and I opened my eyes. "I almost forgot to tell you," he said. "We're invited to Ninka and Vlad's home next Friday night at seven in the evening."

I was excited. I had wondered when we would meet some of his friends. So far we had just spent time with his older aunts and mother and their Old World charm was wearing thin for me. I wondered if being around young people would make me more relaxed with the language, also. My Russian sounded so stupid and stilted when I was trying to impress Piotr's family.

"When you go to their house, you must bring a gift," Piotr instructed.

"Is it a new house they've moved into?" I asked, taking my ice cream to the sink. It had melted into a mauve soup. I thought of Borscht, how I had not yet been able to sample any in my two weeks here.

"No, no. You bring a gift every time you are invited over."

"Mmm. No wonder people don't visit each other much. What an imposition. You're old friends but you must always bring a gift?"

"I think it's a nice custom," Piotr said.

The next day I looked around the tourist shop, the only place that seemed to have items in the open that I could buy. I found a candle in an abstract shape of a blue bear. I asked the clerk in my botched Russian if the gift was appropriate for a household visit.

She shrugged and scowled.

"Well, what do people usually bring?" I pursued.

She made a gesture by her ear like shooing flies. She said something that could have been "it's the thought that counts" or maybe "who thinks of these things?"

"Here, I brought you ice cream," Piotr said the next night, upon coming home from work. His mother was with him and as usual she was full of smiles.

"We should have a meal together," I said, putting the ice cream in the tiny freezer next to the other box of it. "Wouldn't your mother like us to prepare something for dinner?" I smiled back at her, hoping she would relax her series of grins.

"She's eaten already," he said.

We sat in his cramped living room and I struggled to converse in Russian. I felt I was improving at the language, but his mother made me nervous that I would accidentally say something foul or impolite.

"Yes, Piotr has shown the Internet to me," she said. "That is a strange way to meet. We used to meet our suitors at the market."

"Oh, what market?" I asked, eager for information about groceries.

She shrugged. "The only one there is!"

"Tell mother about your job," Piotr said, sitting back in his chair. His change of subject perturbed me. And his idiotic grin made me wonder if smiling was a genetic phenomenon in his family.

"Piotr thinks it's so funny that I work in branding."

"In what?" she asked, her smile widening.

"Well, the brand of a product, its face, its mat of welcome, must be tinkered with, whittled and noodled, so it can adapt to cultural trends, so that folks will feel like hugging it and they buy," I attempted to explain, my Russian coming across as a mix between aristocratic pomp and hillbilly slang.

"And she works very hard at this!" Piotr laughed. "Sixty, seventy hours a week!"

My stomach growled and I felt angry, but he leapt up and sat beside me, hugging me. "Isn't she the most beautiful, most American apple pie little genius you've ever seen?" he asked his mother.

On the way to Vlad and Ninka's Piotr talked about how the evening would go. "We will enter and give the gift, make a toast to the couple, stay for about two hours, then on the way back we will walk along the river. There is a bench I like to sit on under a willow tree. I haven't shown that to you yet. I have crunchy snacks that you haven't tried. You'll like them." His itinerary touched me, as his impulse to plan often did. The way he attached a "where" and "when" to food seemed like rationing, like a scene from a war novel, bittersweet and romantic.

We arrived at the apartment and I gave Ninka the gift. She blushed and handed it to her husband Vlad.

"Isn't she wonderful?" Piotr asked. "She's so giving."

There were six couples including us and everyone was drunk already. I had three shots of unknown liquor before I'd spent fifteen minutes there. I looked around and saw no signs of anything giftlike. No wrappings or ribbons or anything without the tinge of telltale dust. I wondered if Piotr had fabricated the Russia gift-giving custom.

One of the couples got into an argument and the wife went and sat on another man's lap and began kissing him. This man's girlfriend stood at the mantelpiece, seemingly unconcerned by her boyfriend's acceptance of the married woman's advances. The arguing husband went to the mantelpiece girl, whispered something into her ear and touched her breast. They continued to laugh and touch and finally the kissing couple on the chair watched, mouths hung open, at the two at the mantel.

Piotr said, "This is not appropriate for my United States girlfriend to see." He took my elbow and escorted me outside to the stone patio. I waited for him to talk but he seemed sulky. He leaned out over the balcony, crossing and uncrossing him arms on the railing. Finally I complained about the cold.

"I think you should go home to America now," he said.

"What?"

"I'm tired of feeling like a circus act on display."

"That's insane."

"You think of me as the circus bear. That's why you bought Ninka and Vlad that stupid bear candle."

"Piotr," I said. "What happened? Why are you angry?"

"You eat too much. I can't keep up with American women. You always want so much. I should have known that about you."

"I've lost six pounds in two weeks. You won't tell me where to find food."

"You won't listen. You're not interested in the culture. You're not interested in giving effort or time. You want it all pre-prepared. That's why sometimes it's healthy to go on an empty stomach. It builds character."

"I've paid my way ever since I've been here. I brought the gift and no one else bought a gift."

"Everyone knows your economy is strong. It would be rude if you didn't acknowledge that to them."

"It's not my personal economy, Piotr."

He grabbed my shoulders and shook me toward him. I felt my back arch and was reminded of black and white movies. He kissed me harshly. "There. See?" He pushed me away. "Even when I take from you, I feel that you can taste me more than I can taste you."

I went back into the house, letting the door slam behind me.

In the kitchen I had another shot, where Ninka asked me what was wrong. On the computer it had been interesting to poke fun at American mass consumption, I tried to explain to my drunk hostess, but now it seemed to be Piotr's obsession. She nodded, telling me it was Vlad's birthday, and he hadn't received a gift on his birthday since he was a child. They were touched by my generosity, she said. She offered me ice cream and I barked a firm no at her. I told her I needed to get back to bed, to be alone. She helped me into my coat and murmured condolences, but it was clear she didn't understand me. It all seemed to be about a consumption tally, I continued, not caring that she wasn't listening. He could criticize my consumption, and yet his own desires were voracious, I sobbed as the door shut behind me.

Outside on the sidewalk, I heard huffing and gravel crunching behind me. I doubted it was Piotr, because he would be too proud to follow me. I wasn't nervous because it didn't seem like the kind of city where people were mugged. Robbery was for places where people were obsessed with material things, Piotr would say.

I supposed he was right that I hadn't tried hard enough to get to know the city on my own. But Piotr didn't know how hard I had been working in the States, how much I needed to just lay on the couch for a few weeks.

When the footsteps were only a few feet away, I could no longer fight the urge to look back. It was Piotr.

"I didn't mean that. I don't want you to go," he said, taking my elbow.

I yanked away, not ready to make up. We passed what looked like a bakery behind its dirty windows, and I tried to memorize the cross street.

"Good. Because I'm not ready. This is my vacation. And I intend to *take* it," I said.

"So you're satisfied with your vacation? It seems hard to satisfy you."

"It seems that you're the one who's hard to please, Piotr."

"You'll never move here," he said flatly. "It's not good enough for you. I don't blame you. The people are fools: those two couples acting like children. Everybody drunk. They don't have any money, you know. It's why they act like animals. But that's no excuse. I don't blame you for wanting to leave."

"Is that what this is all about?" I asked. I searched his face, which seemed wounded and childlike. I felt sad for him that he couldn't express his worry about losing me without being cruel. But that sense of pity made me love him suddenly too.

He shrugged. "I'm not sure," he said.

We continued to walk, quietly. I felt ashamed that I had chosen to come to Russian in part for a much needed vacation, that perhaps I hadn't considered just how deep Piotr's feelings were for me. The conversations with him online had been intense. There were times when it felt almost real. And yet, there was a realist in me that had never taken it completely seriously.

We passed a man reading on the street. It was past three in the morning and he read by the light of the streetlamp alone. Everyone was always reading in Russia. It was like an addiction. And it made me feel shallow in comparison.

"I want to fall in love with you," Piotr said, "but you'll consume me. And then you'll go back to America. To your sport utility vehicle and rich boyfriends."

Again he tried to hurt me with these cultural accusations. I didn't even own a car.

"I thought we were real people," I said. "Not cliches."

"Yes, so did I. But I know that is wrong now." He stumbled to a bench and fell upon it. "You should never have come. I'll miss you too much when you go."

"Oh, Piotr, can't we wait and see what happens? Perhaps I can stay. Maybe there's a way we can work this out."

He shook his head. "It is this: when you have everything, you can live in the moment. The moment can feel like forever. When you have so little as we have so little in Russia, when you must beg for every scrap, then you must always plan. You cannot accept the illusion that the moment will last forever. Because it won't!"

He was a lovely sight, right out of a Russian novel, his curly dark hair gleaming in the lamplight, the angry way he wiped his wet eyes with the back of his arm. Here was what I had waited for: a boy sick with love for me. It was my dream come true. And while I felt strangely repelled by this living dream, I realized I might regret losing it. I sank onto the bench with Piotr and held him, rocked him. "I won't go," I said. "I won't."

He kissed my face again and again. "I'm sorry, my Michelle. I'm guilty. I was testing you." His sweet tears fell.

The next morning Piotr was ecstatic. "Do you really mean it?" he asked, straddling me, tapping my forehead to wake me up.

"What?"

"You'll really stay?"

"Oh. Yes, yes I'll stay."

"But not just for four more weeks. I mean much longer. The rest of your life. As my wife."

He pulled my hand out from under the sheets and pushed a ring onto my finger. My heart pounded, but my head nodded, before I had the time to think it through.

Well, why not? I had always wanted to live abroad. And he was in love. I had never felt the strength of a man's affection like I felt Piotr's.

"You can't imagine the relief!" he said, tossing his body back onto the bed with a bounce of the springs.

"Relief about marrying?"

"About being able to plan. Of dropping this 'live in the moment' business." He propped himself on an elbow. "I have known, probably since the third discussion we had on the Internet, that I love you and want to marry you."

I was embarrassed that I hadn't felt the same. A big part of me was frightened to be making these promises after only spending two weeks with Piotr in person. I turned my back to him and pulled on a shirt that was on the floor. I thought about coffee, how in America I could go to a café and be alone, but how it was too long a walk from here, and that I might as well drink a cup of tea instead, because Piotr liked the coffee so weak.

"Can I call my mother?" he asked.

"Don't you usually?"

"I mean, to tell her we've made the commitment, that we're marrying."

"Well, yes, but remind her that a wedding really does take planning. I'll want to give my family in the States time to plan their trip here. I mean, we can't do it for at least another six months." I hoped six months was enough time to decide if it was all a mistake.

"OK. OK. But I want to tell my mother!" He picked up the phone.

I couldn't convince my company that there was a need to launch our new product line in Russia. The numbers simply didn't add up, they said. People in Russia were too miserable to see the benefit of a smoking cessation commitment, they said. But I knew I could find some kind of simple job, perhaps at the university, where speaking English was valued.

My mother began to call crying, saying that I gave up too much for too little. "At least he could come visit the States before you make your decision. He might like it!"

When I argued that Russia was a beautiful place, she took on a commanding tone.

"I forbid you to move to a country with so little knowledge about world affairs. You're just across the Caspian sea from Afghanistan, where they make women wear veils — even over the eyes!"

"But mom, what does it have to do with me and Piotr?"

"Afghanistan and Russia have been at a ten year's war."

"It ended ten years ago!"

"So, that much you know."

"Of course."

"It could get ugly. You don't want to be an American in that part of the world. We're very resented."

But I did like Russia. There was a passion to its gloominess. The trains that chugged behind Piotr's apartment building spewed clouds of smoke, like mobile factories. Out his kitchen window I could see the children from the orphanage playing in the yard. Foreign exchange students on the trolley helped me feel connected to a world of hope and productivity. And though they probably couldn't afford it, the young women of Krasnodar always looked fashionable in their smart fur coats and tall boots.

People had lived for romance before. I had always wanted to. Comfort wasn't everything.

Besides, I finally knew where the market was, called the rinoks, and held outside between two large government buildings. Never mind that I hated it — the bins made of dirty wooden planks, holding a tomato or two, an old crone grabbing the better one before I knew she was there beside me. I had located it and couldn't blame Piotr that the vegetable selection was almost entirely made up of roots and tubers.

Piotr was worth it. Piotr in the evenings by the dim lamplight, in the car with the cold wind howling around us. Piotr's skin and his dark curly hair and his deep voice in the night. Always near me during the chilly hours, moving his legs over mine. His moody looks, the long walks in the cold, these were worth everything, every upheaval, every potential change.

But for all Piotr's talk about planning, there was no way to save for our wedding or our future together. One evening he came home and admitted that he was depressed because he hadn't been paid for several weeks. "I'm not sure when the next paycheck will come. But what can I do?"

"Find another job!"

Piotr laughed. "Well, that's nice to think about, but there are no jobs. And if I left this one, I would have to forget about the back pay owed to me."

His mother had taken to her front porch with a basket of produce from her vegetable garden. She hadn't received her pension check for two months. I felt strange buying vegetables from her, but her potatoes looked better than any I had seen at the rinoks.

They lived more day-to-day existences than anyone I knew. It made all this talk about planning more than a little ironic. At least in America there was a way to put money in the bank.

It was cold outside but stuffy in the plane. I assumed Piotr was watching my plane from the gate, but the accordion-like bridgeway blocked my view of him.

Murmurs were becoming more agitated, some angry, as we sat waiting. The plane would not budge. There was a minor mechanical problem that would be fixed shortly, the pilot explained.

I would be home soon. The plan was that I would take care of wrapping things up, ending my lease and packing my belongings, and come back here to this new and different life with a man who adored me.

Things had worked out very well to this point, just by my acting on impulse. Why would I change now? I pictured our Russian children, free of the stifling forces of American television, Russian TV being too boring to watch. Instead they would play outside, in the square, on the massive lawns. Kicking balls. Crying out to each other from their fur lined hoods.

I could still feel Piotr's arms around me. So tight. So insistent. I had never felt this loved. People waited a lifetime for this much devotion.

Piotr and I had imagined it all together, in the four weeks that finished off my stay. How exciting to make plans for the future, to look at apartment complexes where we would start our life together, to talk to his friends about this decision we had made. What relief! To have made the decision, the commitment. To talk about it comfortably because it was already made.

"Don't forget. Bring a lot of panty hose this time," Piotr had said in the airport, kissing me for the hundredth time, pinching my cheek.

The engine groaned. The lady beside me yawned. My magazine slipped from my lap into the bin of potatoes. Now, *here* were some *groceries*. Gleaming aisles that went on and on, their walls of colorful products flanking floors that sparkled like ice. I lingered there in produce, touching each orange, each crinkled leaf of spinach, feeling the pleasant sting of the spritzers as they sprang to life, keeping the vegetables dewy —how ingenious.

Piotr had held out on me, the broccoli said. He wouldn't give. He was the stingier of the two of us, the eggplant agreed, with a wink. Maybe all his talk about my greed, my consumption, was a ploy to distract me from his own selfishness. "You're an American," a chorus of field greens cried from their bin.

The Swiss Chard suddenly began to grow, falling to my feet, expanding into a huge fringed gondola that swept under me, Disney fairy tale music highlighting my journey. I floated past coffee bars where all the ingredients were in stock, past outlet malls where the air conditioning was always just right. Cineplexes with 20 screens showing all the latest releases. I was floating, lifting. Lifting from my doze as the plane's wheels parted from the runway. And out the window the Russian land receded.

Take the Slackers Bowling

JENNIFER BANNAN

Bob has enclosed a check with his letter, a sweet letter that makes me ache for him. I am sitting with Uta at the Co-op Cafe, where she has brought it to me. She's tapping her fingers on the table. I guess she's wondering what I'm going to do. Maybe she's worried about being abandoned. But Uta would never admit to a feeling like that.

"He wants me to come on the tour with him," I say.

"I knew it!" She pounds the table. It wobbles. She throws her head back and laughs, then stops abruptly and looks at me, waits for me.

I'm folding the letter and check together and pushing them back into the envelope. "I'm not going." I slap the letter onto the table and I know she doesn't believe me. She senses a weakness in me—a tendency toward commitment. She suspects that I'm a sorry excuse for a slacker.

It was only a year ago, when it all started. We graduated from the Humanities department of our college, we became vegetarians, we started bowling.

None of us searched for great jobs—there was a recession. Most of us worked as temporaries in offices or as waiters and waitresses in restaurants.

We were the smallest generation of people since those born in the late '30s. This was exceptionally intriguing to us. It meant, on a mass consciousness level, that we were automatically different.

The bowling, I think, was our trademark of dropping out. We bowled furiously, but not competitively; frequently, but with little improvement.

A typical evening. I, pulling off my bowling shoes, sighing: "What's going to happen to us? We're so pathetic." Uta, finishing her last sip of beer: "No, we just have a clue."

We read articles about ourselves in the papers, brainstormed ideas about letters to the editor, laughed at the idea of actually writing something for someone else's paper, and let the newsprint slide to the floor. The older generations called us "slackers." Our parents definitely thought we were slackers. Over the phone, they would ask us how the job hunt was going, holding onto the delusion that there was one. My mother, an early retiree, who called during her rum and coke hour— could always hear "Stock Talk" humming along in the background—wanted to know what my "plans" were with Bob. As if marriage could have possibly been on our minds. There were no plans. We were categorically opposed to any plans beyond, "Bowling, 9:30 Thursday night."

Unfortunately, slackerdom was a hard thing to sell. People either completely understood it and loved it, because they were already slackers, or they didn't, because they weren't. It was impossible to expand the circle, because we could never explain why doing nothing and being satisfied with nothing was valuable. It was the movement of no movement.

Our main motivation was probably apprehension. If you did anything important, we'd reason, you'd probably screw something else up in the process. Or if you did anything important, it might not be noticed, or it might be revealed later as unimportant.

A small bunch of us, including Uta, Bob and myself, were putting together a literary magazine, and we were supreme procrastinators. Everything could be done tomorrow, and everything deserved inane argument. Nothing ever got accomplished. It was thrilling.

The other thing that Uta and Bob and I did, while other slackers were doing their non-conformist things, was bowl. It had become our slacker ritual. So of course we were shaken up when Bob began to really bowl.

Uta, Bob and I all had different bowling schedules. I bowled with him, Uta with him, I with her. Consequently, Uta and I barely noticed Bob's improvement at the game.

Eventually, though, I began to catch on. Bob and I liked to watch Saturday pro-bowling on television. While I made fun of the bowlers' tacky wives and their bad hair, Bob would mumble something about needing a ball with a dull surface. I noticed him putting some of PBA's "Bowlers' Tips" to work later at the alley: a complicated foot pivot, a daring curve. Once when I got mad at him for bowling a turkey, he said, "You should hope I get good. We'd be set for life."

Little things like this were disturbing, but Uta and I were determined not to be swayed from our belief in Bob. He was an upstanding slacker, no doubt. After all, he worked in a submarine sandwich shop, for minimum wage. All day long, he wore a paper hat on his head. In between work and bowling, he wrote poems about hard salami and jalapeño peppers, and above all, he never tried to have them published.

Bob was so skinny and pale and he had a sparse, scruffy black beard. Bob was a silent type, which may have helped to keep us deceived. While Uta and I continued to commend ourselves on our inability to join a crumbling American society, Bob said nothing, Bob picked up his bowling ball, Bob bowled another strike.

Deep into the winter months, I began to bowl very badly. That is, while had I always bowled badly, I became completely incapable of breaking a hundred. I think now, that I was purposely screwing up, but it wasn't a conscious effort.

One night was particularly eerie: In one game I knocked down nine pins during the first shot of every frame and landed a gutter in the second shot of every frame. Bob, however, bowled his high score, a 256. Uta was amazed and thrilled to be witness to such a high score, and I smiled quietly, feeling sick.

That night, I told Bob I didn't think I wanted to bowl anymore. "I'm sick of it," I said. "It stinks of old men and cigarettes and beer and I'm sick of the orange and lime-green color combination, and since I've never gotten up enough nerve to steal the shoes, I suppose I never will, so I quit."

"You're just mad because you're in a slump," Bob said, lovingly rubbing his ball with a soft cloth.

"No, I'm sick of it. It's making my back hurt. I must be throwing the ball wrong."

Bob put the ball in its bag, zipped it in a sort of prissy way, then stood and suddenly lunged toward the refrigerator, letting an imaginary ball slip off his supple fingers. He stood, pivoted, and, pulling back his hooked arm, lunged out at the sink, throwing the ball forward again. I watched him, trying to look detached, hoping he would notice me looking detached.

"No, I really don't think I'll be going any more," I said.

He stood and looked at me, finally. His arm was bent at the elbow, his wrist curled in before his shoulder, as if he were resting the ball on his chest. "You know I won't have any fun if you don't go," he said.

"I know," I said, resting my forehead on my open palms. "I'm sorry," I mumbled.

I peeked out from under my bangs. There was Bob's yellow paper hat on the dining room table. There was my apron, from the restaurant where I worked, rolled up into a greasy ball. There were poems and artwork scattered into disorganized piles; and across all of these things, there was the thrusting, reeling shadow of Bob, panto-bowling.

Uta and I had lunch one day soon after. She had a bone to pick with me for missing the last bowling date we had had planned with Bob. I had gone to a ten dollar seminar on dream analysis instead, which wasn't too bad. My constant dreams about shit (crowds mired in shit, me shitting on myself in public, me going into bathrooms where all the toilets were backed up) proved to stem from my guilt for having to declare only half of my tips for taxes.

"What's your problem with him?" she wanted to know. "Are you jealous?"

"No!" I scowled at her. "That's just it. I don't think he's going about bowling in the right way anymore. I think he's getting competitive."

She laughed. "With us?"

I shifted in my chair. I doodled on the paper tablecloth with the crayons provided by the management. "No. I don't know. With himself, I guess." I sighed.

My drawing was turning out to be a giant turkey with a woman's head. I tried again to explain. "I mean, why did we take up bowling, anyway? Because none of us were any good at it. And we never would be. It was—our trademark."

"Of what?" asked Uta.

"Of being slackers. Of dropping out."

"Oh, dropping out. Well, you know," Uta said, "I don't know that we were ever in."

"Well, I'm just sick of bowling I guess."

"Oh, you are not," Uta said. She leaned back in her chair and looked at me, grinning. "Jesus, it's not like he's going to join a league."

I should probably explain here what Uta, Bob and I had against leagues. First of all, leagues had a schedule, which, like plans, we were opposed to. Secondly, leagues meant competition, inevitably, and competition was against the slacker code. Then, there was the privilege of being in a league. Your lanes were reserved, you were part of an upper crust of bowling. No one else could bowl when the leagues were bowling. Disgusting, thought we slackers. The average guy with the urge to bowl had to wait until the leagues were done, and we thought it best to keep ourselves in with him: the whimsical bowler, the downtrodden bowler, the bowler who wasn't really ever in.

One afternoon in early spring I was taking a shower before work and it struck me that I had been having a dull pain in my back all morning, a pain that shot its way through my torso toward my chest. This seemed to be a pain of some concern, and while I was concerning myself with this pain I realized that what seemed to be big chunks of my hair were falling out of my head by my tugging on them only gently.

Now, I had only been a vegetarian for a little while, and it was possible that the change in my diet was causing gas and maybe a little hair loss. Also, I had a lot of hair, and it was early spring; maybe I was just shedding.

I got out of the shower and toweled off, still concerned with my lungs and noticing my hair loss, when Bob came bounding upstairs to our bedroom. He stood at the doorway of the bathroom. He was carrying a bowling bag. "Look," he said, excitedly, opening the bag. "A steal for thirty bucks at the Salvation Army. It's practically like new and fits my hand perfectly." He picked it up and held it over his head proudly, like a plantation owner might display a bushel of bananas.

"I thought you liked the ball you already have," I said, smiling. I tossed my hair about with the towel and noticed about five strands fall to the tile floor. "Look at that!" I said. Bob looked away from the ball just long enough to *not* figure out what I was talking about.

"What?" he asked.

"Did you see all of that hair that just fell out of my head?"

"No," he said. "You know," he pulled the ball back for a throw and caught it with his other hand as it swooped past his thigh, "a human being loses one hundred hairs a day."

"Yeah, Bob, but this is unnatural, okay? It's just too much hair."

He came into the bathroom and sat down on the toilet seat with the ball on his lap. It was smoky grey with a dull surface, like a chalkboard. He watched his hands move over it slowly.

"And I keep getting this dull, but very—ah, there it is now!—" I pointed at my chest urgently, "this pain going from my back to my chest."

He looked up at me with a mild expression. "Um, maybe you should see a doctor. Listen, there's this contest in Lancaster—"

I pounded my foot on the tile. "Is that my lungs? Is that what that is?"

He shrugged. "It doesn't sound too good."

I felt that I was finally getting somewhere.

"Why don't you go see a doctor?" he said again.

I blew up. "Bob! I don't have any health insurance, okay? I can't go see a doctor!"

Bob got up from the toilet and went back down the stairs with his ball.

"Jerk," I mumbled. It was pretty stupid to yell about health insurance to somebody who didn't have any either. But his easy answers were so aggravating. "You're sick, go to a doctor." As if anything were so simple. And if I had a serious lung infection or something, I could end up with all kinds of bills for diagnosis, medicine, maybe even hospitalization. He could just go to Hell with his easy answers and his stupid bowling ball.

I put what was left of my hair into a braid, dressed for work and headed downstairs. I was pulling on my coat and putting my keys in my pocket and Bob told me about the contest in Lancaster: 1,000 dollars to the winner and a chance for some exposure. Exposure. What did that mean? He was looking at me expectantly while I opened the front door.

"Sounds good," I said. "Have a nice time."

He stopped the door before I could close it. "I was hoping you could come with me," he said.

"You know, where were you today?" I asked. "I saw your hat. Why didn't you go to work?"

"I'm always off on Wednesdays. And since you weren't up yet, I figured I'd go take advantage of the Wednesday practice special at Arsenal lanes."

"Great," I said. "Why don't you just join a league already?

It turns out, my chest pain was gas, and the hair loss was due to a particularly vehement dandruff shampoo. I discovered this through a series of my own tests: not showering for five days and avoiding zucchini altogether.

While Bob was at the contest in Lancaster, Uta and I went bowling. It was the first time I had bowled in two months. I had a genuinely good time, mainly because Uta and I spent most of it bitching about Bob. "You were right. I can't believe it," Uta said, and knocked down six pins.

"It could have been anything though," I said. "Like the magazine. You know how he went on those power trips, how he just knew which poems we should publish, what kind of paper we should print on, what font we should use."

"Yeah, there was no arguing with him."

That night Uta and I came up with a plan. We would come out with the magazine while Bob was gone. Uta had been in charge of collecting all the money from advertisers, and we had plenty of material. We figured, if Bob was going to go ahead and do something "productive," so could we. We published all the material that Bob had been most opposed to, even the stuff that we weren't particularly fond of.

Bob called while we were pasting up the magazine, and I experienced the thrill of lying to him for the first time since we had moved in together the previous summer. "What are you up to?" he asked. "Oh, you know, just hanging out," I said, winking at Uta. "How's the contest?" "Well, I'm doing pretty well. The final round is tomorrow. So far, my high score was a 259 and my low was—"

"Hey, Bob, I'm headed for a movie. Catch you later," I said.

"Okay," he said. "I miss you."

I felt the slightest pang of sorrow.

We distributed the paper all around town early Monday morning, the day Bob was due home. It looked pretty good; the lack of artwork was made up for with some terrific ads. All in all, the writing was only decent.

Just before noon, we stopped into a bar for a celebration drink. "He's going to be furious," Uta said, smiling. We laughed obnoxiously. The bartender gave us a dirty look from the sinks over which he was bent, washing glasses.

We calmed down and I said, more seriously, "I don't want to lose him. I still love him, you know."

Uta frowned. I assume she was disturbed by my conventional use of the word "love."

"Well, I do," I insisted. "You know, I worry. What if he goes pro?"

"Jeez," she laughed. "He's not really that good."

"I don't know. He had already made a 259 in the contest when I talked to him."

"Look!" she said, pointing to a guy sitting at a dark table to the back of the bar. He had a beer in front of him and he was reading our magazine. He picked up the beer and sipped slowly, then paused and raised his eyebrows at something he had read.

Uta and I smiled at each other.

"He snatched that up quick," Uta said. "People are just dying to hear something new."

"Maybe we should have waited for Bob," I said, feeling a little guilty.

Uta started to say something, then closed her mouth and leaned into the bar.

"What?" I asked.

"No, I was just going to say something, but—" she wrapped her hands around her beer. "Hey, you know what some guy told me on the bus the other day? He said that my name rhymes with bitch in Spanish. Then he starts going, 'Uta Puta, Uta Puta.'" She laughed and shook her head, looking down at her beer.

Bob came home from the contest with a thousand dollar check and a trophy with a little gold bowler on top. He had bowled a 281 in the final round, blowing everybody else away. I was very disappointed at his response to our coming out with the magazine. He thought it was great that we had finally gotten something accomplished, he said. He didn't so much as groan at our inclusion of the poems he hated most.

Then Bob started getting calls. He got new shoes and a bowling bag and three new balls, all different shades and of various sheens. He started going to more contests, and eventually, on tour. Uta had trouble with her landlady, and since I was lonely and had lots of space, I invited her to move in.

That was about two months ago today.

I spend a lot more time these days in my room, remembering what life with Bob was like before graduation, when we spent all our time together at lunch and in between classes and in the evenings over beers. We talked about our plans for the future, when we thought we might actually get jobs and go to work and in fact go to work *somewhere really cool* and do art on the weekends. And we would sometimes sit under a sprawling willow tree and actually talk about what we would name our kids. The campus was so massive and pristine and it wasn't that difficult to think of it as an estate that belonged to us, because we had been such important artists who had given so much to society—we deserved it really. And since that was a silly fantasy, it wasn't so hard to say later that we didn't need all that or really want all that, that we didn't need the good jobs either, or the acceptance of our parents or the peace of mind that comes with health insurance. But nowadays, in those moments spent hiding behind the door of my bedroom, behind the cover of my flimsy, frayed bedspread, I know that throwing away all those plans for the future never meant throwing Bob away. And I would do anything to be dreaming with him again on the campus, hearing his gentle intellect, his steady-as-she-goes, reasonable acceptance of opportunity.

And maybe Bob feels what I'm feeling now. Like: okay, being a slacker is fine, but is it worth throwing away all possibilities, all commitments, all plans?

Now Uta and I leave the Co-op Café. I stuff the letter from Bob into the back pocket of my jeans. The weather is gorgeous, but Uta has an indoor activity in mind.

"Bowling?" she asks.

"Okay," I say.

It's early afternoon and only one lane is taken. Of course, the management sticks us right next to the only other bowler in the place. "There's a league at four," says the guy at the desk. Uta and I roll our eyes at each other.

We get our favorite balls and sit down to put on our shoes. Then we both notice the guy. He's about our age. He has a small build and a Buddy Holly hairdo. But what's getting our attention is the way he bowls. He starts only three feet from the penalty line and looks intently down the lane over the curved surface of his ball. Then, he takes roughly fifteen of the smallest, most gingerly taken steps I've ever seen, lets the ball down slowly and opens his hand gently, giving the ball one tiny shove. It rolls down the alley in slow motion. It curves dangerously toward the right-hand gutter, then just as dangerously toward the left, then back toward the middle, just in time to hit the pocket, between the first and third pin. He never looks away from the lane. He keeps his eyes fixed on the ball as it makes its slow journey toward the pins. He wills them down with the power of his mind, I think.

When Bob bowls, the pins act as if they have happened upon a land mine. When this guy bowls, it is like a mercy killing. All the pins subject to imperceptible, merciful gas: they collapse in a grateful heap.

We watch him bowl. We watch an entire game. It is incredible. He almost always bowls a strike or a spare. Finally, Uta turns to me. "I'm in love," she whispers.

And, while I am too, I can't help thinking of Bob, and his beard scratching my face, and his yellow paper hat perched on his head like a fat canary. How lonely he must be on the tour, with no league stories to tell, no coach stories, or bar brawl stories. They're probably picking on him: he only bowls with a fourteen pound ball.

Maybe I've been unfair with Bob, I think. Watching the intensity of the slow bowler's style, I have to admire Bob for being so involved in something himself. And then I'm getting up and walking past the desk and Uta is yelling "Where are you going?" and the desk clerk is chasing me and I'm running through the swinging doors, down the stairs, around the building, down a back alley and I stop to catch my breath. I rest my palms on my knees and let my head hang forward.

I've finally done it. I see on my feet, the red and green, soft and supple shoes I've always wanted, but never had the nerve to take.

Fear of Heaven

JENNIFER BANNAN

It's her. Little Sam. Two years later and there she is in the back of my classroom, her hands small and waiting on her desk, a finger rising and falling in random rhythm. Sam's ears are delicate and ready, processing whatever rustle or whisper surrounds her. She waits for me, Mr. Pavord, third grade teacher at Miami Beach Elementary, to teach. She waits like the other students are waiting, and the chalk feels fragile in my fingers, as if it will crumble into fine sand, lost to us forever, lost like those days when Sam and I knew each other well.

I remember the night at DeLuca's, April 1997, the night when I met Sam's father, Ron. I was tired of the club scene and Ron was venturing into it for the first time in a decade. Our relaxed conversation was out of place in the throbbing bass of the house music, and we kept bumping heads as we tried to hear each other over the noise. We decided to head for more common ground, elbowing our way past leather boys and good jawlines.

We got outside and walked up Collins Avenue to a Chinese restaurant nearby. Palms tossed above us and headlights streamed by. Every now and then someone would honk, a little late, like a lazy afterthought.

"I'm used to the Hot and Blue Lounge," he said, and I felt the rush of adrenaline course through me.

"I play at the Hot and Blue sometimes," I said.

"I know. The trumpet. I wish I were good enough to play in public. But there's not much demand for mediocre Jazz pianists."

As we settled into a bright red booth, I was reminding myself not to fall too hard. And I wouldn't rush to bed with him either, I decided. I figured he was twenty years older than me—the kind that can get needy fast. He grabbed my hand over the tabletop and rubbed my knuckles. "Trumpet players have the best knuckles. It's all I can see when a guy's playing the horn."

"I'm a sucker for the pianist's pedal foot," I said.

"If the shoes are good," Ron added.

I pressed closer into the glass tabletop. It loosened and slid suddenly toward him, pinning him back. We laughed, straightened the glass and sipped simultaneously at our tea.

"Wingtips are the best," I said, but Ron looked puzzled. He'd already forgotten our train of thought—the shoes, the pedal foot, all small talk, who cared? I knew he was forgetful of the conversation because so much else was skidding through his brain, like mine; the air was charged between us.

His eyes made me think of soaked grains of sand at the beach, a million atoms crushed together. His cheeks were creased with the best laugh lines I'd ever seen—long and deep, like dimples, but mature.

He talked about his six-year-old daughter. His voice seemed to dip on the mention of her name, Sam, like the thought of her was a gully he savored falling into, would keep falling into all his life.

He was married to a woman named Kathy.

I asked if he had known he was gay before he married.

"I wanted to be a father. And it took four years before we had Sam. Sex with a woman wasn't the biggest motivator, you know?" He laughed and so did I. "But the time went by fast. We stayed involved in our work." He was a director for a small foundation for the blind, he explained, and Kathy was a partner with the city's top law firm. "She's very committed to her career," he said.

"Does she know?" I asked.

"No," he said, shrugging.

"Why now? Why are you going to the clubs now?"

"God," he laughed and shook his head. "I'm lonely for something more than family, you know? I guess I'm lonely."

We headed for the beach. It was like a black-and-white movie in the dark, in the moonlight. We walked the curves and heard it come and go, roaring in our heads, rippling over our feet. Ron pressed a porous fortune cookie to my palm and crushed it. I felt the paper unfold and the crumbs fall away. We held the paper up, trying to catch some light, but instead it caught the wind. It fluttered away from us, small and doomed above the waves.

I look at Sam today, this first day of class, August 1999. She sits at her desk and stares me straight in the eye, with complete recognition. Of course she knows me. I wonder if she knows the whole story, though.

I remember the day after Ron and I met, how funny I felt in the classroom, trying to teach Florida history. Look at that hat, I wanted to say about the metal helmet on Ponce de Leon. *What a vamp. He's dressed for a rave.*

Every five minutes the urge arose to call Ron. Finally I gave in and called him at work. I got voice mail and left a silly message, imitating Marian McPartland, public radio's piano lady, saying I wanted him to play a little tune on my show.

He called me that night, late. Ron hadn't dated for ten years. I was the first guy he'd been with since getting married. "I didn't really expect to meet someone nice right away," he said.

"Thanks for the stellar compliment," I said.

He laughed and said it was his bad habit. "My friends are: 'nice,' the trip to the mall was 'nice,' the neighbors' new Suburban is 'nice.' I've turned into a boring guy who wants to escape to the clubs, but feels out of his league there. Thanks for saving me at DeLuca's. I was about to leave," he said.

Then, over the line, I heard the piano. "I can play if I keep the damper pedal on," he said, and I pictured his big house on the posh side of Miami Beach, his piano in a room on the far end of his house, his wife and child sleeping at the other end. He played music for me, every once in a while stopping to talk some more.

We saw each other all the time for about two months, when one school holiday just before summer break, over croissants in bed in my apartment, he said he wanted me to meet Sam. "You'll love her," he said. "She's daddy's little girl and she takes the job seriously."

We went to the zoo together that week. I was worried. I knew that it would bring me closer to the reality of my situation: that it would make me realize the depth of his involvement with this woman, his wife, with this little girl, his daughter. Part of me wanted to avoid thinking of them. I didn't want to know the Ron who could walk down a wedding aisle with only procreation in mind. I rationalized that he was older—from a time when gay men couldn't have families unless they practiced deception.

As much as I didn't want to like Sam, though, I did. She was serious, the type who would grow up to be bookish, the type I would love to have as a student. Sam reminded me of her father, except for the pigtails, and something else—a grown-up brand of impatience that I supposed came from her mother.

"I'm starting first grade in September. At the school where you teach," she announced to me, first thing, a tinge of lisp in her speech.

"It's a great school," I told her. "You're going to love it."

Sam nodded as though I hadn't provided her any new information. She pulled on Ron's hand, and he grinned at me as we entered the zoo gates.

Sam was obsessed with ears. She wouldn't let us look at an animal without considering the creature's auditory system. "He has pointy ears," of the chinchilla. "He has round ears," of the tiger.

"Yes, like your Fuzzy Bear," Ron said, and the familial reference hurt me somewhere hidden but vital.

"You know," I ventured, as Sam ran ahead of us to the flamingo pool, "speaking of ears, hearing and speech are related. You might want to have her tested."

"We have. She's been through routine tests and her hearing's excellent," he said. It was the first time in a while I'd heard him say "we" without meaning himself and me. "She'll grow out of it. Look at her reading the information on the flamingos," he said, and she was indeed standing before the backlit kiosk, head cocked, as interested in learning about the flamingos as she was in seeing them. "She's amazing."

I didn't say anything else about Sam's hearing. We stopped for hotdogs and cotton candy and I talked to Sam about the animals we had seen. She had an uncanny catalog in her head: she could remember every animal in the exact order seen. I found it fascinating, if not a little intimidating. I imitated the baboon and she squealed, seeming truly childlike for the first time that day. She bugged her eyes and licked her lips fast, clapping when I guessed she was monkey. She begged to go back to the see the monkeys after lunch.

I caught Ron, enraptured, obviously happy that she and I were getting along.

At the monkey house he stood close behind me. I watched Sam crouched at the glass where the baby gorilla rolled his black furry body. Just the glass separated her hand from his fur.

"This has been great," he whispered to me from behind. All the contentment of having me and Sam together that day was warm in his voice, warm as the glass must have felt to her fingers where the baby's belly pressed flat. "I love you," Ron said. It was the first time he had said it, and his chin was on my shoulder.

"You're really great with her," he sighed, like he was giving up, satisfied. And I was happy too, to know Ron, to understand how his being a father added to the depth of his personality. How could I blame him for wanting to be a family man, when it was in his nature?

But then I saw her turn, the recognition of her father's voice showing in her face. Had she heard? I wasn't sure. But I was suddenly concerned with the vibrations in the coils of her peach-fuzz ear, echoing and spiraling and possibly being processed into meaning. Maybe it would be her first realization that her father wasn't truthful to her mother, a realization that might entwine itself with whatever future struggles she would know. It was an unfair world that allowed children, so unprepared, to discover the betrayal of the ones they loved. I didn't want that for Sam, and from then on I would encourage Ron to avoid overtures in her presence.

But as it would happen, that wasn't enough. The truth of Ron's betrayal would haunt me.

It was guilt that nagged at me, I knew. I was a teacher, and I liked children. I knew I might be helping to break up a home. I knew that wasn't fair to Sam. But then, I reasoned, Ron had set it up this way. His lies to his family were his responsibility to fix. I hoped, now that I had fallen in love with him, that he would commit to living for love, instead of living for stability and appearances.

My friend Jane, who taught the Level 3 sixth graders, came into my classroom after the bell and sat at one of the tiny desks in the front row. "So, tell me about the new guy," she said. She wiggled her pinky finger in her ear and I shuddered.

I looked at my desk. "He's great. But he's married."

"Well, it's the nineties. People make all kinds of arrangements."

"I don't know. It doesn't feel like quite the ideal arrangement. It's arranged just right for *him,* if you know what I mean."

"Women are used to it these days. Name a woman who hasn't been dumped for a man and I'll give you a dollar."

"There's a kid in the picture though," I said.

She shrugged. "Who can make sense of it?" Jane asked. "If you were a woman, I'd advise you to drop him. Sure, he doesn't love her, but he's a heel to cheat. He made his bed. He should lie in it."

"It's weird how she always calls you Mr. Pavord," Ron said, looking at the horizon, checking from time to time for Sam's bobbing head in the ocean.

I laughed because I hadn't even noticed. Children always called me Mr. Pavord. In front of the kids, I called all my colleagues Mr. or Mrs. Something. It was elementary school culture.

"Well, once she gets to school, that's what she'll have to call me anyway," I said.

We watched her come to shore and begin digging in the sand, her body bent in stiff efficiency as she worked the small shovel.

We had been going to the beach almost every day those two weeks I had free between full term and summer school. Ron would get out of work around four, pick Sam up from daycare and then head over to my place. We'd walk down to the shore and stay till sundown. For Sam's sake, we had been playing up our buddy status to the hilt, complete with hearty pats on the back and booming laughter. It was ridiculous, but it was easier for both of us that way.

Sometimes, though, I would forget, let my guard down, laugh with Ron in a way that only lovers laugh—only to see Sam yards away, her head cocked, listening.

What had she heard? Was she cataloging our conversations—however hard we tried to couch our language—was she saving the information for a more mature time, when she might decipher it? What did she understand?

"What does your wife think about that tan?" I asked Ron now.

"She likes it," he shrugged.

"Do you think Sam will ever figure out our relationship?"

"No," he said, and I could tell he had thought about it a lot.

We had just finished making love and I knew Ron had sensed a preoccupation in me.

"I feel like she knows about us," I said. I thought maybe, if I could solve the issue of Sam knowing, our relationship could evolve normally. "It's not fair for her. She expects a family where her parents are in love. And she thinks we're these great pals. I hate lying to her."

"She's six, Gary! She doesn't understand," he said.

"It's such a big lie, Ron," I said to him. "I'm a teacher. I love kids. And this is such a big lie to tell a little kid."

"She'll probably run into bigger lies as she goes through life."

"Eventually she'll have to know you've lied to her and her mother so long. She's going to know."

"You should meet Kathy. You'll see that she's absorbed with her own things. She would never suspect," he said.

"What, am I going to become friends with her? We'll be manicure buddies? Come on, Ron."

"Kathy doesn't have to know you're gay," Ron said.

"Oh, so maybe I can come up with some fake girlfriends. Hell, maybe I'll marry one and have a kid."

"Being a father is the best thing that ever happened to me," he said, irritated. "You don't understand the depth of that feeling. It's not the same as having a strong relationship with one of your students. Even if Sam learns that I'm gay, I know she'll understand and love me. It's unconditional with your own flesh and blood."

"No, it's not. Open your eyes. All around the world there are children who don't speak to their parents," I said.

"Sam and I have a special relationship."

"She won't like finding out that you never loved her mother. That you never loved women."

"Really? What about the fact that I sacrificed my entire love life for *having a daughter?* What about that?"

"But you didn't! You're not sacrificing anything! Look at this!" I grabbed at his arms, threw a leg over him. "Look."

I tried to show him the bed, the sheets, the fact that we were naked and had been making love minutes before.

But his face registered nothing. And I realized that Ron had forgotten he was cheating. He had been so successful at compartmentalizing his life that he didn't look at his relationship with me as cheating on anyone.

I stopped touching him. "Unless being with me is nothing serious to you. Maybe being with me means nothing," I said.

"No," he said, crumpling. "I do love you." His hands came to his face. "But, all the skulking around, hiding— that's a struggle that I go through for Sam, because I want her to have a happy childhood."

"It's all getting too complicated," I said. "Sam will start first grade this fall—at my school! Kathy will start coming around. Who knows, Sam might even be in my class when she reaches third grade. I can't take this. I can't let our lives get wrapped up like this. Not with this huge lie hanging over us."

"I'm sorry, I don't know how I can change it," Ron said. "I don't know how to get out. I'm messing up your life, and I'm sorry."

"You know, being gay and having a family is possible. We could have that kind of life together."

"I don't think things are that progressive," he said. "Maybe things are different for your generation. Maybe you'll be able to be true to yourself. You're just thirty. It might work out for you."

"Maybe it could work for us— together."

"I could never take Sam from Kathy. She would win custody. The fact that I didn't love her but married her and stayed with her all those years. That alone would make her case."

"What about having our own family?" I suggested, knowing it wasn't possible.

He was true to Sam. How could he not be?

I watch Sam break away from her science project group, walk over to the bookshelf and pick up the conch shell that lies on top of it. She holds it to her ear, cradling it, swaying back and forth. I think about telling her to get back to her work, but the memory of a smaller Sam – at the beach, in just this pose – rushes over me like a suffocating tide.

When I was with Ron, I thought a lot about the shells Sam picked up on the beach. A shell is like the outer ear, I decided, gathering sound for no one; laying forever in vibration, with no inner ear to sort out the data. But now Sam makes me wonder, does a displaced shell still vibrate with memories of the ocean? Or does it begin to store and hum with the sounds of its new environment?

She turns slowly, still holding the shell to her ear. She turns and looks at me. She nods slightly, as if she's taking in some important information. She has gained some of her father's patience, I realize. She will wait for my approach.

I dreamed of the three of us together, escaped to some tropical island, Sam running up the beach with sand on her round little limbs, bringing us shells as gifts.

When I wasn't fantasizing, I worried about it to my friends, who I saw at work now that summer school was back in session.

"Are you concerned that his wife will find out?" Jane asked.

"That's part of it. I think it's bigger too, like I think it's awfully callous to marry someone just because you want a family," I said.

She peeled her orange, lazy and slow. "Yeah, I've known men who want it both ways. They want to be gay but they want to have children, so their wives are just completely in the dark. Or they leave their wives when the children are grown. It does seem wrong. Do you think he would leave her once Sam is grown?"

"Yes, I think that's his plan. I love him and I think about waiting, like the good little mistress. I think how happy I would be to be with him alone, but—"

"But it's what bothers you about him. That he could have such a cruel plan," Jane said.

"That he could have had the plan all along, on his wedding day, when he was having sex with her. . . ."

"You wonder what ulterior motives he has with you," she said. She pushed a lock of hair behind her ear. Light came through the window behind her, causing her ear to blaze red. I looked away.

Summer school classes ended at noon and Ron took frequent half days off, which we continued to spend at the beach. Sam liked to sit next to me on the beach blanket and pat my face and pull at the hair on my chest. Sometimes she would bury my feet in the sand and then screech in delight as I rumbled them out of the ground. Then she was up, jumping and running, barely dry from her previous swim and ready to plunge in again. The days were at their longest and Sam spent hours in the water, giving us plenty of time to talk in private.

"Doesn't she mention me at home?" I asked.

"Yes, but Kathy thinks we're buddies," he said. "It's one reason I think you two should meet. She's surprised she hasn't met you yet."

"No thanks," I said.

"Mr. Pavord!" Sam called, running up to our blanket. "Mr. Pavord, I found a seashell. Maybe I'll sell it, like 'she' did!"

She passed the shell to me and we recited tongue twisters, which sent her into giggles as she faltered.

"She sells sea sha shahaahahah," she gave up, laughing, and tickled me, the skin of her arms cool in the hot sun. She patted my face and grabbed my ears.

I caught her wrists. "Hands off!" I said, flipping her onto her back and tickling her wriggling body.

Ron was reviewing a grant proposal for treatment of scotomaphobia, the fear of going blind. "It's ridiculous the things people want money for," he said, throwing the papers onto the sand.

"Will you give it to them?" I asked, watching as Sam ran up the beach to a group of girls about her age. I loved the sweet dance of children interacting, the intimacy and shyness marking every movement.

Ron shrugged. "I prefer to help the already blind than those who can't get off their bums and appreciate their vision."

That night I was curious to learn more about scotomaphobia, and I looked it up on the Internet. The phobias list was much longer than I expected.

There was so much uneasiness in the world. It was amazing the things people were afraid of. Obscure fears, but common enough to be named: of the Chinese, of chins, of being looked at, of taking a bath, of theaters, of beautiful women, of clothing, of the color yellow.

One phobia that intrigued me was Uranophobia, the fear of heaven.

It occurred to me that I had a fear of heaven — the heaven of being happy. I couldn't take the pure pleasure of Ron without obsessing over who else we were affecting. People everywhere were taking love wherever they could find it. Why couldn't I? Why did I have to care who we might hurt?

INVENTING VICTOR

It wasn't two weeks after classes had started again and we already had a lice epidemic. Principal Chumbley came into class and asked that all students clear their desks. "We're going to check your hair for lice. Don't worry. It won't hurt," he said.

He asked me to come over to his side as he stood behind Brittany Taylor. "Did you forget we were doing this?" he asked me under his breath. "Your kids all had their permission slips signed."

I mumbled that I may have been putting it out of my mind.

"Put your head down on your desk," he told Brittany and then he turned to me. "We're short staffed today, so I'm hoping you can watch and learn." He pulled from his pocket tiny thin sticks and used them on Brittany's long hair, like a chef separating udon noodles. Then he got to her left ear and used the little sticks to fold it back.

"Here you go," he said, handing over the sticks. We moved on to Juan Carlos, who put his head down eagerly. Chumbley smiled at me, nodding, "You'll need to take care of your class. I've got to get to all the other teachers today and show them how this is done. Just report any kids with lice to me."

Juan Carlos's hair was thick and very black. I moved through it quickly, trying to pull off an out-of-body experience, imagining myself on the beach, taking in sun, digging my toes into the warm sand.

But those days were all but over. It was full term school again, and we were usually too busy for the beach. Sam was in the first grade now and every morning I watched from the teacher's lounge window as Kathy dropped her off under the huge banyan tree near the school bus driveway. Sam spent her days in the first grade building, just a patch of grass away from mine. I often passed her in the lunchroom as her class came and mine went, but I usually pressed my finger to my lips, and this kept her from bolting line or calling out to me. It seemed secret smiles had become our only means of communication, and I hated their similarity to Ron's lies.

"Good, but make sure to check behind his ears," Chumbley said, catching me before I could move on.

"I, uh—"

"It doesn't hurt them," Chumbley said.

I looked around at the students watching and wondering what made me hesitate.

"OK," I relented, moving in with my sticks. Then a, behind Juan Carlos's ear, appeared a grouping of lice, scurrying for cover in the black hair, where they stood out like fugitives under the spotlight.

"Uh," I said, handing the sticks back to Chumbley. Something was wrong. I just couldn't make it through this exercise. "I don't feel well. I think I've got food poisoning."

I edged to the door.

Chumbley watched in amazement. The sound of my students turning in their chairs was maddening, a low scraping. "Be good for Mr. Chumbley, kids," I said, getting out of there.

I went home that day and got under the covers. I pulled the blinds and slept the morning away.

Ron and Sam came over that afternoon for the first time since summer's end. I didn't say anything about the lice incident. I put hats on both of them and we headed to the beach. Somehow I was able to enjoy my afternoon with them, but I had the feeling that something within me had changed.

Almost as soon as we laid our blankets down, we noticed dense clouds appearing on the horizon. In less than twenty minutes it began to rain, and we scurried up the blocks from the beach to my place. The sky was dark and the wind whistled through the jalousie windows in my apartment. Ron decided he wanted to make stuffed shells for dinner, since Kathy would be working late again that night.

Sam and I sat at my piano and plunked around. I played the few songs I knew. I wasn't any good, but Sam enjoyed it. The light in the house turned Italian grotto green, and Ron's clanking and dinging from the kitchen and the delicious feel of Sam's impatient little fingers on my hands gelled together into the ideal of family. I wanted it then as much as Ron must have wanted it all his life.

And I told myself *take it take it take, don't fear this slice of heaven.* I told myself that if Kathy found out, that would be my dream come true. Ron could move here and we could play music and we'd get Sam on weekends and I should *take it.*

He served us with a flourish at the table and we laughed around pockets of cheese and sauce and tongue twisters. The rain poured steadily outside and Sam's feet swung back and forth.

But then the wind blew one of my balcony doors open, knocking over the palm I had been planning to move for about a week. The door cracked against the back wall and a pane of glass broke free and shattered. The small tree crashed onto the piano in a jumble of discordant notes, then rolled across the bench and landed on the floor. We looked at it, soil and glass everywhere, fronds splayed unnaturally flat on the hardwood. The rain blew into the room. I jumped up to close the door, but some impulse seized me and instead I went to Sam. "It's OK," I said. "Don't worry." I smoothed the hair around her face. I pulled her toward me for a hug.

"I'm not scared," she said, pushing me away gently. She looked at her father, "Can we go home now?"

"You've still got some dinner to finish," I said, my hands around her wrists seeming more pathetic by the second.

"Sometimes I just want to have dinner at home," she said, glancing at her father again.

"Come here, Sam," Ron said from behind me.

I felt foolish holding her. I went to the door, closing out the rain and propping the palm up again.

"Don't you like the dinner I made?" I heard Ron ask her.

Sam spoke quietly, as if she didn't want to hurt my feelings, "I want mommy."

"Of course, darling," I heard Ron saying as I crouched over the shattered glass. "I want mommy too." I turned to see Ron looking at me over Sam's shoulder, his eyes full of apology, an apology I could no longer accept. I shook my head and looked at the shards of glass in my hands, the tiny bead of blood forming on my thumb. Ron had no illusions about family. To him, family meant the constant sacrifice of the truth.

The conch shell sits on the bookshelf in my classroom. I hold it to my ear, but I don't hear the ocean. I hear the sound of children whispering. They whisper about the world that hums up next to them, bumping them from time to time, sending them to each other, to make meaning out of the world's humming.

When they're very small, children hate to share. But as their world becomes more complicated, they learn that sharing is a comfort instead of an imposition. Sex worries them and they go to each other about it. Their worry brings them closer to sharing, and the sharing brings them closer to their worry. They only scrape the surface. They come to understand the working parts. They grow older and they try to make sense of love. They'll never make sense of love.

That next evening, a Saturday, we walked the beach in the twilight and I couldn't decide how to say it. We walked by the many families who had been out in the sun all day, staring frankly in their tiredness. I wondered what they thought, if they assumed we were brothers.

"Sam," I said. "Please go find a pretty shell. I need one for my classroom." She looked doubtfully over her shoulder at her father but obeyed me.

I looked at him and I could see that he knew what was coming. "I know you're happy with the way things are," I said. "But it's too hard for me. And it's cruel to Sam. I didn't think it mattered at first. I believed you did what you had to do. But, I'm sorry. It's not enough. It's not enough justification."

"Shhh," he said, his face set in a pained smile. "Don't explain anymore."

We went behind the lifeguard's booth and he looked around. There was no one on this part of the beach. Sam was directly behind us, blocked from view.

He kissed me deeply and long and a pressure built in my nose and forehead and when we let go we were both crying. We looked at each other for a long time, saying nothing.

"It's been a long time, hasn't it, Sam?" I ask now, at this moment, in which she is packing up her bookbag, in which she is the last student in the classroom.

"I knew I would get your class," Sam says. "You have the smart kids."

"How's your dad?" I ask.

"He doesn't have many friends," she says. "I think he misses you." She looks right at me, then heaves her bookbag over her shoulder and walks out the classroom door.

I think maybe he was right, maybe their love is deeper than anything I would ever know. Maybe she knows that I was her father's lover. Perhaps she can accept this betrayal of her own mother in a way that I can't.

I'll continue to go to DeLuca's where the nights are a string of house music beats and I have yet to meet the person like Ron, the man who wants the togetherness, the children, the quiet closeness. I don't know why Ron's wife takes this blessing for granted and I don't know why I should care about jeopardizing it for her.

I feel like a shell. Like an ear. Gathering and storing but never getting to make any sense of it. There is no meaning, I think sometimes. There is no answer for the roar of the sea.

The Bruise On Jupiter

JENNIFER BANNAN

She had raised her hand to her children. Using that phrase, Leah could reflect on her wrongs, in her room, in the silence of her Brooklyn apartment at night. She knew it was worse, though. It was bad enough to cause her to lose her children, and bad enough that she was exiled from the Hassidic community. But when her mind explored the past much further than those consequences she lived with now, the phrase went up like a shield: she had raised her hand.

Images sometimes forced themselves in: bruises on her daughter's arms, bloody scrapes on her son's cheek or burns on his baby soft skin. The flashes of her own pain surfaced too, like the surprise of her stinging palm long after the anger was gone. It amazed her that she could have hit them hard enough to make the sensation linger on her own skin.

She remembered begging the children, begging God later as she lit the Shabbos candles. She wanted to believe it didn't hurt so bad, to believe that her hand was stinging for some other reason, from cutting the peppers for dinner – her skin was allergic to peppers, did they know that? They didn't care about her allergies, though. They never thought of her, always licking their own wounds, as if she never felt any pain herself.

Now the pain was a constant, a truth wrapped up in the inescapable memory of their sweet skin. Baby skin was soft like nothing else.

Her children belonged to another family now. And that family belonged to the Hassidic community that had failed Leah, the community that hadn't protected her as promised — not from her ex, not from American law, and not from herself. The Hassidim always shrugged dismissively when it came to man's law, concerning themselves only with God's law. But they leveraged man's law when it suited them to do so. Like when her sister-in-law had said terrible things in court about Leah's treatment of Marta and Joel. Leah was shocked by the words that came from the woman, who she had treated like her own sister, who had so many children she couldn't even afford to fix the stupid problem with her teeth, so that the air whistled through all the spaces in her mouth when she talked. They had connived to get her children away from her—into the community and out of her hands.

Leah was done with the community.

When she met Ian, she believed she could start over. She had met other men these past months alone in the world—but none yet had caused her to believe she could begin a new life. Ian was real, though. He wasn't playing with her mind. She took one look at his face, over the book she handed him, recommending it in the Judaic bookstore, and it was like a door opened. "I like your taste," he said. "Let's have dinner."

"I was married," she told him over scallops in wine sauce. It was her first time having shellfish, and the graininess seemed to prove everything she'd heard about bottom-dwellers, but there were a lot of things she was leaving behind, lots of hang-ups of the ancient religion that had only caused her misery. So she took another chewy-crunchy bite, tasted its sweetness and all the sin it represented.

"I'm sorry it didn't work out," he said.

Ian had no reaction when she ordered the scallops. Food rules were not part of his Judaism. In fact, he seemed to follow none of the Jewish laws, and she wondered how he could really consider himself a Jew. She hardly considered *herself* a Jew anymore and daily she marveled at the pain and relief that realization brought her.

"He escaped to Israel. He's gone. Good riddance. He used to beat me. Good Hassidic man and he beat his wife." That was true. She hadn't told any lies yet.

"I can't imagine a woman like you being beaten by anyone. A strong woman—you seem very strong."

"I am strong! The things I've been through." She laughed. "I'm like a suspension bridge, all strength, from one side to the other, one life to another."

He smiled. "Maybe you're too strong for your own good. Maybe you're inviting people to drive over you."

"Yeah, but this bridge has speed bumps. They know it when they've driven over. It changes them and next time they know enough to slow down."

She enjoyed talking about herself this way. No one had ever cared what she was like before. And here was Ian eagerly awaiting her next description of the way she felt.

"My daughter changed me. Made me slow down," Ian said, mentioning his daughter for the first time. Leah felt the scallop catch in her throat. She felt suddenly nauseous. She hadn't been ready for scallops—who was she kidding? She spit the meat into a napkin and gestured to the waiter.

"She spends the summer with her mother in Florida," Ian continued. "When she gets back I hope we can be together. You and Molly would really hit it off."

"These have gone bad," she told the waiter and he took the plate with many apologies.

Leah smiled and shrugged at Ian. On second thought, his having a daughter was good. Maybe he wouldn't want more children—certainly Leah wasn't supposed to have them. Leah liked the way he talked about introducing her to Molly at the end of summer, an entire month away. It showed that he expected to continue dating her.

"You should be sterilized, Leah," Aimee, her social worker, said. Leah believed Aimee loved her, despite everything. She believed Aimee used painful words because sometimes those were the only ones that made it through. They sat in Aimee's tiny office, so small that Aimee looked like an advertisement for tissues, with the Kleenex box on a shelf touching her shoulder.

"There's got to be a chance I'll get back the baby. At least baby Ruven," Leah said.

"No," Aimee nodded sadly, took her hand. "You've made too many mistakes."

"The adoptive family makes mistakes too. Don't they ever have to pay for their mistakes?"

Every time she had a visit scheduled with the family who had the children, they managed to cancel. How was this legal? How did they not get into trouble? It threw Leah into fits of hysteria, kicking the walls, throwing and breaking ashtrays, screaming alone in her apartment. Her daughter of nine years, her son of five, her one-year-old baby she had never touched with her fingers, her baby she had felt only as he left her womb. The family had full custody now, in their Jewish ghetto, with their ultra-Hassidic self-righteousness and their holidays even Leah had never heard of. It was over.

If Leah had another baby, it would be the same thing. There was no redemption. All the Saturdays, all the prayer, wouldn't change this. No one in the community would help her. She was an outcast.

The last time she had gone to the synagogue was for a wedding. One of her ex's nieces was getting married. Leah had been skipping Saturday shul, because she suspected the Hassidim would now want her to return to the Orthodox community she had come from. But after nine years with the Hassidim, she knew none of the Orthodox, and didn't see why she should start over. An Hassidic wedding — a time of joy — she thought it would give them an opportunity to welcome her back, if their hearts had softened toward her.

Leah was late, and when she tried to edge up to the wall separating the men and women, to look over the side at the bride and groom at the altar, the women stayed tucked close together, shoulder to shoulder. "Let me in," she had whispered to her sister-in-law, the one who had testified against her. But the woman must have recognized her voice, because she would not budge. Eventually Leah gave up and looked at the backs of their heads, each like the next, in a black wig with a patch of lace on top. She had considered a plain, black wig that morning, but thought it would flag her desperation to belong, and would be dismissed as too little too late. She had chosen a stylish, dirty-blonde wig, like many modern Hassidic women wore, and the kind this community was accustomed to seeing her wear. But the reality was that, her wigs might have been a slight aberration before, but today, with no children, and no husband on the other side of the wall, the wig sealed her fate as a complete outcast.

No one wanted her here. They had let her in once, forgiving her Orthodox background and its relaxed laws, partly because of the marriage to one of their men, and partly because her parents were dead and they pitied her lack of family. But the Hassidim had no time for her failures. They had no time for a woman who couldn't keep her children or husband. She had left the synagogue before the ceremony ended.

She couldn't even pace in Aimee's small office. She was like a trapped animal. "One year I've not touched my third child."

"You cancelled some of those early appointments, Leah. You know I'm fighting to get better visitation," Aimee said, pulling at Leah's sleeve.

"No! That's not good enough. To never have touched your baby—I'm sorry, Aimee, but you don't know what that's like. That family is not honoring visitation, so the State of New York should do something about that. They owe me another chance."

"You will not get Ruven back. And if you're thinking about another baby with this new guy, I'll warn you. New York will make it very hard. They'll be breathing down your neck," Aimee said. She took a tissue and blew her nose.

She hadn't really believed they would take Ruven. She knew a social worker from Youth Services was in the waiting room. But the way the doctors and nurses encouraged her, "You're doing a great job, great job, very good, Leah! One more push." She heard them cheer her on and she just knew the misunderstanding would be smoothed over and the hospital staff would let her keep him. She saw his purple face lift up, his red gums pulsing with that first wild cry. "He has so much hair," she cried with joy, and then the stitched cotton back of a nurse blocked her view of him, and he was gone. She hadn't seen him again.

Ian didn't sense this loss. Her lost children, her lost community, her lost religion. She didn't want him to know, because it would ruin things. He was the only part of her life that was about possibility.

Saturdays, they drove to the shore. The freedom was beautiful—she savored the elevator trip down to meet him, the feel of his hand on her bare elbow, the roar of the car engine and the wind in her uncovered hair. Though she had been breaking Sabbath rules in her apartment for months, it was quite another thing to break them in public.

Only the food laws lingered with her. She didn't say a word when they stopped at the non-Kosher diner. But she couldn't mix milk and meat yet. And the sight of bacon on his plate made her feel dizzy. She picked up the newspaper and hid her distaste behind it.

Ian knew she had married into an Hassidic family, that her husband had abused her. To Ian, the abuse alone was reason enough to leave the community.

She had more reason than that, though. If she had done it her way, she would have left town with the children, she would have taken Joel and Marta to Israel the minute there was trouble with the police. But so many people in the community told her to play by the rules, to stay calm and state her case. Then some of them turned around and testified against her. They tricked her and now her children were in the custody of a sect so strict that at visitations she was treated like a leper.

When she thought back on the years the community had turned their back on her husband's crimes, the years they had treated her with disdain for bringing home a paycheck when her husband refused to because of his prayer schedule, and then the way they had called her a criminal in court, she realized that she liked almost none of them. She considered most of them to be hypocrites, liars and provincials. And yet she felt frustrated to be cut out. She often fantasized about reaching out to the community again, returning to knock on one of their doors, perhaps that of Lillian Werrin, a successful business-woman in the diamond trade, who was different enough from the others to have something in common with Leah. She missed Mrs. Werrin.

Mrs. Werrin also had assured Leah that no one would take her children, that her crimes were because of her husband. But as they all sat through the testimony, listening to the things her Goy neighbors said, listening to her sister-in-law recount the day at the playground when Leah had raised her hand to Joel, Leah became frightened that Mrs. Werrin would leave before speaking in her favor. When Mrs. Werrin testified that she had seen bruises on Leah, she did not sound like the confident, strong woman she was; her voice was meek and she fiddled nervously with the brooch on her lapel. Leah was filled with shame that Mrs. Werrin had lost faith in her, but strangely she didn't feel anger for the woman. More than any others in the community, Mrs. Werrin had made some effort on Leah's part, so Leah could forgive her. She could imagine Mrs. Werrin giving her a second chance.

"You don't seem too uncomfortable getting out on a Saturday," Ian teased her, flipping through selections on the tiny jukebox affixed to the wall of their booth.

"I'm not done being Jewish. I still read the Torah," she said, folding up the paper and setting it aside.

Ian was happy with the way she was – he didn't need more explanation for her rejection of Hassidism. "Sadly, I'm more capitalist than Jew," he laughed.

There were so few forbidden things with Ian. Life was pleasant with him—and without the community. Alone in her apartment she had been lighting cigarettes on Saturdays for six months already, making the forbidden spark, but it felt so much better doing it with a cohort, a lover who drove on the Sabbath, keys sparkling in his hand as he turned the ignition. She put her fingers on the car radio knob and felt the satisfying click. They sang the old Motown songs, laughing and stealing glances at each other.

They made love in the back seat, on the side of the road, her skirt hiked up. She looked over his shoulder at the road stretched out and thought how so much was behind her. Too much for anyone to experience, but perhaps she'd made it through.

"You should tell him," Aimee said. She could feel Aimee's heavy sigh fill the small space.

"And if I don't?" Leah said. "You wouldn't, would you?"

"No, I can't do that."

"Well, I can't either."

How could she tell him even half of it? The state took my children from me and my husband. The community failed me, even testified against me. Even though I hated my husband, I conceived another child with him the day they ruled against us. They had already taken Marta and Joel, but that wasn't enough for them. When I gave birth to Ruven, they didn't even allow me to touch him. I want to start over. I still believe I deserve a happy life.

Why should he think she deserved anything after a story like that?

"I hope you're using birth control," Aimee said.

"Of course I am."

Leah and Ian waited at JFK baggage claim for Sara, Ian's ex, who would return his daughter to him. They appeared, and Ian ran to them, his long legs loping along.

Molly was a ten-year-old with dark Sephardic curls and a mouth like a heart-shaped candy—so much like Marta. By the time Leah had caught up with them, she found that she couldn't control the tears.

"What's the matter?" Ian asked, rising from hugging his girl.

Sara looked at them with confusion.

Leah gasped and said, "I'm sorry. It's good to meet you," she thrust out her hand. Sara took it but let it go right away.

Ian said, "Molly, I want you to meet my friend, Leah."

"I always want to cry at the airport too," Molly said with grown-up empathy.

Later, she lied. "She's like my little niece who I haven't seen in so long," Leah said, her body against Ian's in bed, her emotions raw and possessive. "She's yours—a little you. And I'm so crazy about you. I was overcome."

Ian turned and pulled her close. "I can already see a connection between you and Molly."

"I didn't think anything could be this easy, after everything I've been through," she said.

She listened to his breathing become regular. He fell asleep like this every time, the moment his head hit the pillow. Even when he was awake, though, he never asked about her past. So often she found herself holding a detail in her mind, ready to hand it to over to him, only to find that he'd moved on.

Tonight she remembered the bruise on her cheek, the nasty one she had gotten before the neighbors had started calling Youth Services, back when Joel was just a baby. She remembered how the bruise had reminded her of the spot on Jupiter, how when she touched it she thought it might as well have been that far away—on Jupiter. Her skin had nothing to do with her. Her husband had been out of the house for hours, probably praying with the others, studying the Torah. How she had hated him for praying with the men like a good Jew. She hated them all at that moment: Joel in his crib, screaming, his head lolling. Marta hiding behind the sofa. Had she shaken Joel? She was afraid to go back in and look at him.

She stood at the mirror and looked at the bruise. She hated him praying in the shul, never doing anything but praying and beating. He didn't even bring in an income. She was the breadwinner, using her degree in accounting, when all the while the community criticized women who worked. But he allowed her to break the Hassidic laws when it suited him.

She worked hard every day and hoped that the children would be happy to see her in the evening, but often they were scowling or crying. They never acted as though she made them happy. She didn't know anyone who seemed to like being around her.

Suddenly she hadn't been able to take the sight of the bruise anymore and she headed for the hallway to the baby's room, striding with an overpowering purpose she couldn't explain.

"No!" Marta screamed, tearing into Joel's room, pulling at Leah's skirt. In the crib the baby protected his face with his crossed wrists. Leah saw this and fell into the corner on the stuffed animals and screamed. She shoved an animal's paw into her mouth and felt the dusty fur turn her tongue dry. She wasn't sure how long she had sobbed there or what had stopped her this time. When she had calmed down, Joel was standing in the crib watching her with large wet eyes. Marta had collapsed onto the floor with her mother, and was now stretched out, her small head and curls next to Leah's ankle. In the darkened room, their skin glowed. They were so beautiful, and she kept hurting them.

She was alone with Molly one Saturday when Ian had to travel to a conference. If Aimee knew, there would have been trouble, since Leah wasn't legally permitted to spend time alone with children. It was a beautiful day, very warm for late September. They went to the petting zoo, sat on a park bench and ate ice cream, bought hair accessories at a little store in Chinatown.

The sun was probably too much for a child to take in for so many hours, though, and when they returned to Ian's apartment, Molly was irritable.

"I hate these hair clips! We shouldn't have bought them. They're terrible."

"You liked them in the store," Leah said, taking off her shoes and rubbing her toes. She hadn't walked that far in quite awhile and her feet felt as though pieces of wood had been shoved between the tendons.

"*You* liked them. You were so sure they were the right ones. You were pushing me." Molly was perched on the hall table, turning her head back and forth in front of the mirror.

"Get off the table, Molly."

"I think you were in a hurry. You were probably bored."

Her grown-up tone was horrible, and Leah dug in her purse for a cigarette. "God, you sound just like Marta," she mumbled around the filter, turning the wheel on the lighter again and again without a spark.

"Like who?" Molly turned and looked, derision and scowl on her perfect little face. "You shouldn't smoke around children. I don't have fully developed lungs yet."

"Fine!" Leah yelled and threw the lighter. It hit the mirror and made a sound as loud as a shotgun. Before it hit, Leah was up, to quiet it, to stop it, but instead she was yanking the crouched and frightened Molly by the arm, off the table. She heard the yelp of pain as the shoulder socket was strained. In the silent moment that followed, the air conditioner groaned into motion, and that was just enough to cause Leah to stop and watch herself. She let go of Molly's arm.

"Go to your room," she said. Molly rubbed her shoulder and went down the hall, her skirt swinging vigorously.

So that was it and that was short, Leah thought, getting on her hands and knees to reach for the lighter under the table. Molly would tell Ian and that would be the end of it.

She always let things go too far. It was like the time her ex had come in for the hearing about Joel and Marta. She sat in the meeting room with the social workers and judge and her ex across the table from her, and she could barely look at him. Her head seethed with hatred for him, fresh as if she had seen him the day before, when in fact he'd been out of her life for six months already.

But then after receiving the bad news about the children, he had hugged her in the hallway; he had cried. Twenty minutes later they were at the apartment, conceiving Ruven. She should have known not to let her guard down with him. If she was alone with him it was either sex or fighting. But she had needed a man right then, and perhaps, having just learned that she couldn't keep her children, she had needed to get pregnant.

She had made a lot of mistakes. That was true. Still, the circumstances of the past had been too complicated. She knew she could do it right if she started out completely fresh, with all the right circumstances in place. She took her cigarette out to the balcony and leaned over the rail, fondling the impatiens in Ian's flower box. Upon close inspection the petals seemed to glitter in the sun. She closed her eyes and realized that, with the right touch, the petal felt like the sweet skin of a baby's hand.

Molly was already out of her room when Ian got home that evening, and she acted normal around Leah. Her shoulder didn't seem to bother her either.

Later he was tucking Molly in and Leah waited, sitting dressed on the side of his bed, ready for him to ask her to go.

"What are you doing?" he asked, coming over and kissing her.

"Zoning out, I guess," she laughed.

After they made love, she asked him if Molly had mentioned the argument.

"Yes. She said she was being a brat and that you probably hate her now."

Leah had to turn her head from him to hide her pleasure. "I think she's wonderful. Everywhere we went today people commented on what a lady she is."

"My ex can be a witch too, so I'm glad Molly's inherited Sara's better genes." His voice was becoming heavy with sleepiness. "I'm so sorry that you aren't able to have children."

"What?" she sat up suddenly. "Why do you say that?"

"I'm sorry," he sat up too, flicked on the light. He looked at her with such kindness and worry that she relaxed immediately. "I assumed, because you were Hassidic. And they have so many children, right away they have so many."

"Well, he was beating me. My body probably refused him. But I'm sure I could — with a man I love."

"It was a lousy assumption I made," he said, ignoring her hint. He kissed her and turned off the light. The apartment creaked and moaned around her, reminding her of how fortunate she'd been that afternoon with Molly, to have had the house interrupt her anger.

The next morning, a Sunday, she snuck onto Ian's balcony to call Aimee on her cell phone. "Are they there?" she asked. The meeting place was just a few minutes away, walking distance from Ian's apartment.

"I just got a call on my cell. They say that Joel is sick and that the baby has an earache. They say no one can bring Marta."

"Whatever happened to going to their house, Aimee?"

"You know what they say, that your presence is disruptive. That it's hard on the children."

"Goddamit!" Leah yelled, then checked behind her that no one had heard. "What's our recourse? They can't keep doing this."

"I've filed some complaints. I'm sorry, Leah."

Leah entered the quiet apartment and began making coffee in the kitchen. The grounds scattered from her shaking fingers. She pressed her palm on the countertop and felt the jagged edges of each grain.

They would always act like this—like they were above the law. It wasn't only that they ignored visitations. They also wouldn't be permitting Marta to finish high school, because the family that adopted her belonged to a sect so strict that girls were expected to marry, not to consider getting a job or going on to Yeshiva University like the boys. Leah wasn't sure if it was against the law to force a child to drop out of school early, but it certainly seemed like it should be. Marta would never be able to leave the community if she wanted to, having no skills to support herself. Whenever Leah fantasized about Marta coming to find her, she realized the girl would probably never leave the ten-block radius she lived within now.

Joel no longer spoke English and certainly couldn't read it. What kind of school was this? Leah had asked the social workers, but they insisted that this was the only family they could find. She had been the one to originally request a Hassidic family, they reminded her. And it was true she had made that request, because she had committed to the Hassidic life years ago, had made sacrifices for that life, and had not intended to ever leave it herself.

But the last time she had seen Joel he had acted like he didn't know her. The foster mother shrugged and frowned, sweeping the floor around Leah's feet.

Now Leah's baby Ruven was lost to her too, growing so fast miles away from her. They disregarded the visitations like formalities they couldn't afford. Like customs that didn't apply to them.

Ian came into the kitchen and kissed the top of her head. She scooped the coffee grounds up and tossed them into the sink. She watched him hunched at the open refrigerator, yawning and scratching his chest. She loved the simplicity of his life, the way his needs and emotions were out in the open, the way he had nothing to hide.

Her period was late and she was usually regular as clockwork. If she were pregnant, no one would be pleased. But Leah was. She was pleased.

"They've agreed to a visit," Aimee said over the phone.

Leah sat on the toilet, looking at the positive pregnancy wand. She had let a month pass, ignoring the morning sickness, ignoring her sore breasts, ignoring everything but her ability to be loving to Molly and Ian. "I have to call you back," she said into the phone.

“OK,” Aimee sounded uneasy. “I thought you’d be excited. It’s the Sunday after next.”

“I am. I’m just in the middle of something.”

“Well, can I tell them you’ll be there?”

“Yeah, but they’ll just cancel at the last minute anyway.” She hung up.

Ian would be at her apartment in fifteen minutes. He was picking up bagels after dropping Molly off at school. He and Leah had plans to skip work together—a morning date.

She looked at the plastic wand in her hand and considered crying over the certainty of it. That would be dishonest, though. She had done it on purpose.

She wanted that baby moving inside her. Her fresh start. Her new baby.

She had spent so many days alone with Molly. Nothing had happened, except the day with the hair clips, nothing had happened. She was cured, now that she had a new life, now she was divorced from the abusive husband and the obsessive people with their five-thousand-year-old religion.

For the first time since the baby was taken from her, she allowed herself to think about her relationship with God, to believe that he was rewarding her for what she was learning. She glowed with the feeling that He had noticed her progress with Ian and Molly and was showing trust in her, with this new life.

She wanted to touch that baby skin, smell that baby hair. She wanted another chance. She yearned to tell Ian their news, but how could she explain that they would have to escape? Because she couldn’t stay in New York, with Youth Services watching every move, blowing every little thing out of proportion, always threatening and demeaning her.

She and Ian would have to leave New York and go – where? Israel, she thought, and that was crazy, like going back in time.

She was just an American now. And Americans escaped to Canada or Mexico. Since Canada would be too cold, it would have to be Mexico.

Ian rang the bell and Leah buzzed him up. She greeted him at the door with a huge kiss. She took two steps back and waved the wand in his face. "Surprise!" she said.

Ian laughed, then focused on the wand, his face becoming serious. "Not the greeting I expected, Leah, to tell the truth," he said, taking the pregnancy wand out of her hand and holding it at his side, as if to hide it. He looked around at her things like they belonged to someone he didn't know.

She was panicked at his reaction, his rejection, but then just as quickly she felt relieved, and she knew she would have to lie. After all, if she had his baby with him, Ian would have to learn everything about her. She believed he loved her, but he would hate that she had deceived him for so many months, that she had allowed him to trust her with Molly. There was no way to explain her situation and then expect him to uproot his life, to hide from the law, to live thousands of miles from Molly, with a child abuser raising his new baby.

"Oh, it's just a joke. I'm not pregnant," she said, taking the wand and bag of bagels from his hands and turning toward the kitchen.

She never should have told him about the baby in the first place, she realized, and threw the pregnancy wand into the trash.

"You're not?"

"No, two lines means negative," she laughed. "Thank God. I want to have children one day, but only when I'm trying to do it!" She put all her energy into slicing the bagels.

Ian kissed the back of her neck and went about readying their breakfast. She was disgusted by his composure, by his ability to sail through life with no interest in what lurked below the surface.

She had told him only for the most selfish reasons, only for the possibility that he might be joyful. She hated herself for her desperation. She spent too much time wanting people to be excited and happy to be around her. She hated herself for wanting it again and again, when clearly that wasn't how people felt about her.

But that was to be her fate. With her gift from God came one more punishment: that she and her baby would always be alone, no one happy to be near them.

The morning glittered like a jewel, brisk and bright with flashes of blue and many sides to consider. She walked past the banks of flowers at the market, the strange sea life wriggling in shallow pans of sparkling water, the peanut vendors, Latin music store and the strong fishy smell of the leather shop. Her life as a non-Hassid in New York had been brief and she longed to stay. She longed to experience the city in freedom for a few more years, but that was not an option.

On the way to the diamond district, she walked under Aimee's office window, wondering if she would see her friend again. There was still the possibility of the visit to her children.

Seven blocks later, at the Werrin house, she rang the bell and was buzzed up.

"Mrs. Werrin," she said, taking the woman's hands.

"Oh, Leah, everyone is wondering where you have been!"

"I'm easy to find. Just ask Youth Services." She was embarrassed by the bitterness in her voice.

"We didn't turn you in. The Goyim complained about you first. If even half of it was true, Leah, you were very wrong." The woman's words were harsh, but her hand, stroking Leah's hair, was gentle. Leah's throat was closing already, preparing for the release of tears that Mrs. Werrin's attentive hands inspired.

"The community said everything would be fine, but all my children have been taken from me."

"No one betrayed you as much as you betrayed your children, Leah. You were supposed to care for them, and instead you beat them."

Leah looked at the door. She could leave, she knew, but there were things she needed from Mrs. Werrin.

"I feel sad that you lost your children," Mrs. Werrin went on, removing Leah's coat. "I can't know that pain. But Leah, the beatings, the constant cruelties, so many visits to the hospital," Mrs. Werrin said.

"I raised my hand to my children. It's a terrible thing to do," Leah said, trying to quiet Mrs. Werrin.

"Leah," Mrs. Werrin led Leah into the sitting room, sat Leah onto a brocade ottoman and stood before her. "Leah, you brought your hand *down* on them. Again and again. And not just your hand. Your pencil, your fork, your fist."

Leah saw it in her mind. The things that Mrs. Werrin described, she saw the flashes of those things before her, as though on a movie screen, and she wasn't sure if they were memories or imagination.

"I'll get some tea," Mrs. Werrin said, leaving Leah alone with her anxiety. Something was different hearing the story of her actions now. It had been a long time since she had heard someone speak the words that described what she had done to the children. Mrs. Werrin's voice made the images seem very real, and the realness made her feel as if she was crumbling or melting. It was a horrible feeling, and she worried it would paralyze her here in Mrs. Werrin's apartment.

"Why didn't you come to me and talk to me about this sooner?" she accused Mrs. Werrin when the woman came into the room with the tea kettle and cups on a tray.

"What?" Mrs. Werrin's eyebrows rose, large, strangely hairless brows. The items on the tray clattered and trembled as she settled her burden onto the coffee table.

"It's too late for me to think about this now," Leah explained. "There's something else important to attend to."

"What? What could be more important than atonement? Think of the prayer for rain. The temple priest, 'In prayer he raised hands, cleansed, sanctified in water.' That is raising hands, Leah. Raise your hands in prayer."

Her focus had been on the wrong things, Leah realized, and she felt ashamed to tell Mrs. Werrin about the new baby. Her focus had only been on what she wanted, not on whether she could be trusted with that dream.

"I suppose I have to leave town this time," she cried, then took a deep breath and told Mrs. Werrin everything.

"I'll help you," Mrs. Werrin said. "You pray to God, and I'll help you."

Leah's throat closed again, and tighter. She was overcome with emotion that Mrs. Werrin wanted to give her another chance. She ached for the community, even though they had betrayed her. She imagined herself and Mrs. Werrin, living comfortably in this elegant apartment, with the new baby growing up strong and beautiful and Jewish.

"You were always a little different from the other women in the community, Leah. A little bit like me," Mrs. Werrin said, pouring Leah another cup of tea.

"But you succeeded and I failed. I can't stay in the community like you have. I must leave everything."

"Yes, well, pray that God will make you gentle with this new baby."

So Leah asked for what she needed. New papers, new identity, some money, all the things to which the Werrin family had access. Of the entire community, the Werrins were the most adept at skirting the laws of man.

"Often travelers are tempted to pray for good weather. But you must pray for rain. Pray for a cleansing rain."

Mrs. Werrin assured Leah the things would be ready in two weeks. Then Leah could schedule her airline trip.

She got back to her apartment and fell to her knees, sobbing against her bed. She was tired of her past, but her future seemed like a futile struggle. When she thought of Mexico, she imagined leaky shacks and cockroaches crawling like an army over the chubby limbs of sleeping children, the limbs of her child.

The phone rang and she let it. It would be Ian. He had been calling for weeks. But she was done with Ian.

"Leah," he said on the machine. "Pick up."

He waited and then said, "Please call. You have to call me."

She rarely thought about things ahead of time. She did what she wanted, like most of the Hassidim, who felt laws didn't apply to them. It was a hard feeling to shake – that of being above the laws of man.

But she was even worse than the community. At least they still followed the laws of God. She did exactly what she wanted and now here she was, faced with exile again, from her city, from the possibilities of future visits to her children.

She pictured Mexico again. The shack, the crying baby, the water that might not be safe to drink. With all of those irritations she knew there was a chance she might lose her temper, that she might raise her hand to her child.

No. The fact was, she might slap her child's face, her baby. She might twist the chubby baby arm, hard, until hearing a snap. She might put the baby's hand in a door and close it, turning the fingers blue, breaking tiny bones. Fresh tears soaked her cheeks. Because she might push a fingernail into the baby palm, slicing until the cries were hoarse and contorted in the baby's mouth. She might pull out tufts of the baby hair or lift the baby up by the ears.

Mrs. Werrin was right. Leah needed to face it, to stop this blaming of everyone else. She needed to look it in the eye and beg God's forgiveness. At Yom Kippur she had said the prayers of atonement, but only as a formality. She hadn't been ready then to think about God. Now, now that she had no choice, she got on her knees and she asked God to show her. To show her her sins, no matter how painful, and then wash them away.

Aimee stood waiting beside the park bench. Marta, Joel and the baby sat beside the woman they now called mother. Two other children, probably the woman's actual offspring, stood behind the bench. Aimee nodded at the woman, who nudged her black wig, picked up Ruven and handed him to Aimee. She then took the two children by the hand and walked with them to the fountain about fifty yards away, where they sat and watched.

Marta, Joel and the baby looked at Leah with no emotion.

"Hello, Marta," Leah said, moving quickly toward her daughter with a wrapped gift. She extended it and then impulsively hugged the girl. The edges of the gift cut into her ribs and must have done the same to Marta, who whined and squirmed away.

"My goodness, you're so big! And you too, Joel!"

Joel had a curious smile on his face, amused but not trusting, as if she were a clown entertaining him. She reached into her purse and gave him a present too. The two of them let the gifts lie on their laps.

"Joel said he couldn't remember you," said Marta.

"Well, now you know who I am, right, Joel?" said Leah.

He giggled and covered his face. He seemed far too childish for a five-year-old.

"I guess you don't speak English anymore?" she asked him in Yiddish.

He raised his eyebrows to a comically high level and then said to his sister in Yiddish, "How does the Goy know how to talk?"

Leah was stung. Her knees screamed from crouching. She stood and looked at the mother at the fountain, with her black wig and her bad posture. Leah had worn long sleeves and a long skirt. It was the hair that made Joel say that, the uncovered hair. That, and the more painful truth – he no longer saw her as his mother, or even as a relation.

Suddenly Leah was filled with fear of looking at the baby in Aimee's arms. She could hear him struggling against Aimee to get down, to walk. He could already walk, Leah had learned from Aimee a few weeks back.

She turned and looked at Aimee. "Well, thanks!" she said, trying to wrap things up.

"Here," Aimee said, furrowing her brow and holding Ruven out to her. He was large, dark and hairy like his father, squirming in the air. Leah was overcome by a superstitious feeling that if she touched him, she would drop him. She wasn't capable of holding him. She would drop Ruven, she felt it very certainly. Then she would be detained, her pregnancy would soon become apparent, and her chances for happiness would be destroyed.

"No." Leah took a step back. "No, I can't."

"What?" Aimee practically yelled.

"I have to go," she said, quickly kissing Marta and Joel, feeling their soft skin on her lips, turning away, not looking back. She walked with control at first, but soon found herself running.

She could not save the past. There was no sense dabbling in anything that could jeopardize her chances with the future. She needed to get control of her future.

Mexico was stupid, for one thing. Leah imagined other cities, cities that also had fountains and paved streets and all the good things about New York, everything but social workers and people who knew her. She should stay in the States, a nice mid-Western town where no one from New York would find her.

No, Mexico had been a bad plan and she needed a better one. She needed to think and to think hard. She saw Ruven clearly in her head, a baby, hers but not hers, suspended in the air, fat face, arms stretched out straight. She had wanted to touch him all this time. And, finally, given the chance, she had been afraid of herself. She was afraid for the child within her too.

Perhaps God had forgiven her. Perhaps God trusted her with this new baby, this gift. But she did not trust herself. She had only eight more months to learn how. But how would she learn, she wondered, now that she had no one? She stopped, gulping air, turning in slow, dizzy circles like a pigeon, like a pathetic, diseased bird, a bird who waited for the rest of the world to keep it alive.

She had a lot of work to do. One conversation with Mrs. Werrin wasn't enough to change her. One night begging God's forgiveness was good practice, but not enough.

She was far from cleansed. She deserved a beating rain, a downpour, brutal, stinging, cruel, with drops that sliced as deep as her nails into their soft baby skin.

Carnegie Mellon University Press
Series in Fiction

Fortune Telling
David Lynn

A New and Glorious Life
Michelle Herman

The Long and Short of It
Pamela Painter

The Secret Names of Women
Lynne Barrett

The Law of Return
Maxine Rodburg

The Drowning and Other Stories
Edward Delaney

My One and Only Bomb Shelter
John Smolens

Very Much Like Desire
Diane Lefer

A Chapter From Her Upbringing
Ivy Goodman

Narrow Beams
Katie Myers Hanson

Now You Love Me
Liesel Litzenburger

The Genius of Hunger
Diane Goodman

The Demon of Longing
Gail Gilliland

Lily in the Desert
Annie Dawid

Slow Monkeys and Other Stories
Jim Nichols

Ride
David Walton

Wrestling with Gabriel
David Lynn